THE MAGICAL MYSTERY CRUISE!

A CRUISE BROTHERS NOVEL

RON COLLINS

JEFF COLLINS

SKYFOX PUBLISHING
Science Fiction

The Magical Mystery Cruise!
A Cruise Brothers Novel
Copyright © 2024 by Ron Collins & Jeff Collins

Songs:
"Frisky" © Jeff Collins & Ron Collins
"Let's Disappear" © Jeff Collins
"Sabrina Katrina" © Jeff Collins
"I'm Back, Better Than Ever" © Jeff Collins

Cover Design by Ron Collins
Cover Image: @yogysic

This book is licensed for your personal enjoyment only. All rights reserved. This is a work of fiction. All incidents, dialog, and characters are products of the authors' imagination. Any resemblance to persons living or dead is purely coincidental. This book, or parts thereof, may not be reproduced in any form without permission.

Skyfox Publishing

ISBN-10: 1-946176-71-0
ISBN-13: 978-1-945176-71-4

For Kate and Brigid

The Cruise Daughters!

PROLOGUE

"Gargh!"

Fae Feral groaned as she blasted out of the lift tube and onto *Marvel*'s observation deck.

"I'm going to kill him," she sighed. "I am literally going to kill him."

Her active-array stage outfit glimmered with refracted starlight as she wrapped her six-fingered hands around the railing that lined the deck, enjoying a satisfying moment of ecstasy as she imagined the rail as the neck of one Altair the All-Knowing. The deck was empty now, as silent as the deep space vacuum that lay outside the viewscreen. Her chest heaved with exertion, and her heavy breathing echoed in the open space. Running down a cruise liner's hallway and ducking into a lift tube could do that to a person.

The observation deck felt sterile.

A hum radiated at frequencies so low she could only pick them up if she dropped a proper earbud follicle. Outside, at the periphery of the view panel, the Cygnus

Grand Central loading station sat in silence. A few hours remained until the captain called general boarding, so the deck was a place where she could be alone.

She'd had enough, though.

Enough of the rejection. Enough of the auditions. Enough of the condescension that came from perky new entertainment directors who thought they were doing the world a favor simply by existing. Enough of the assholes like Altair the All-Knowing groping their way through the business.

She and her sister Doozie had played gigs on Galactic Cruise Line ships before, back when they were fresh faces, just starting out — including a stint on *Marvel*. How ironic was it to come full circle? The more you change, the more you stay the same, as they say where she came from.

I just want to go home, Fae thought as she stared morosely into the darkness outside the window.

The huge spacecraft was docked, and preparing for another tour: *The Magical Mystery Cruise*, they called it. It should have been a fun jaunt. What better place to be a shapeshifter than a cruise liner full of magicians, after all? The whole Feral Sisters act was based on what other people considered to be illusions. The sisters were thrilled when the cruise lines reached out to book them in support of Altair the All-Knowing, a legendary magician perceived by his cultic followers as half-mystic and half-philosopher. He was headlining the cruise and would draw people from parsecs around.

The Feral Sisters would assist Altair, as well as play a side stage in a second shift. Doing two gigs at once would be exhausting, but the chance to ratchet up their profile on the biggest cruise tour of magicians in existence was worth it.

A good review on this ship and maybe they could grab a top billing someplace else.

They didn't, however, need a breathless young cruise director to tell them this could be their big break.

Now, though, she had come from pre-launch rehearsal with the cruise's Guest of Honor, wherein she discovered Altair was nothing but a full-bore horny snout. Fae had shot him down, and not in a particularly kind way.

Now everything was ruined.

She drew a clean breath, gave a blistering sigh, and pressed her forehead against the cold surface of the portal. To keep her hair out of her eyes, she resorbed strands of the wild mane she'd expressed specifically for the rehearsal. The velvety vacuum of space lay dark outside. A star pattern glittered in icy shivers that made the sequins of her sarong pulse. Pressure dissipated in the quiet moment. She closed her eyes and let the moment settle in.

Shapies—as people in this part of the galaxy called her and Doozie—were rare. But that was partially because this part of the galaxy was full of assholes, like Altair the All-Knowing. Being a shapeshifter meant dealing with people who mostly didn't understand that she and Doozie weren't just some kind of infinitely configurable set dressing.

The lift tube whisked open behind her, and her sister stepped out, also still wearing her stage get-up. Her expression was as dark as Fae's but more resigned than outraged.

"It's all right," Doozie said, putting an arm around her. "We'll be fine."

"No, Doozie, we won't be *fine*," Fae said. "We will never be *fine* as long as there are idiots like that around —and there will *always* be idiots like that around." She drew another ropey appendage from her right side and pounded it hard against the deck's flooring.

"Be careful, love, or you'll crack us open to vacuum."

"The skeezy letch." She chewed her lips. "He only hired us because he wanted to *try out* a shapie."

"Men." Doozie twined a tendril of dark annoyance and looped it around her sister's shoulder. "Always so handsy."

"It's not like he couldn't have had whatever he wanted if he'd just asked first. He's not even horrible to look at."

"So true," Doozie replied, tilting her head in the affirmative. "Neither one of us has ever been that picky."

"They gotta ask, though," Fae snapped. "No breaking personal space without asking. At least not without some kind of warning."

"Forewarned is foreplay."

Fae took in the distant star pattern outside the cruiser. With Doozie here, her anger had fallen to a slow simmer. "He won't even let us use our names on stage."

"That does suck."

The small print of the contract had required that Fae and Doozie take the names Sabrina and Katrina while supporting Altair's act. On the face of it, the clause was there to maintain the show's consistency as Altair

THE MAGICAL MYSTERY CRUISE!

played across the galaxy, but they both knew it for what it really was. The asshole didn't want anyone to be able to upstage him, so he gave everyone generic names.

"Are you Sabrina, or am I?" Doozie said.

"You're Katrina."

Exasperated, Fae blew a new lock of hair from her eye.

The tour was a four-planet hop, with the marquee destination being a free-space jaunt through the ion clouds of the Horsehead Nebula and the chance to do sub-atomic mixing with a newly forming star system. *Be part of history! Feel atoms before they come together!* The opportunity had been exciting.

"I don't know, Dooz, we've been doing this gig for a long time and where has it gotten us? Maybe it's time we shitcanned it all and went back home. I'm sure I could get my old job back at the Multi-Q Gravity Lab, and I know Dr. Benobcall would love to have you back under his wing."

"He'd want me under more than his wing."

"Sure, but he's very good to look at, and … um … also very bendy." Fae laughed, recalling their time with Lyn Moore, the human guitar player from the Intergalactic Band of Brilliance who had called them that.

He'd been cute enough, if silly.

The Moore Brothers would be on this cruise, too, which had been an attraction of sorts for Fae and Doozie. Their Intergalactic Band of Brilliance was becoming a big name — and even had a novelty hit with their song *Frisky*. Even better for them, they were always getting into the news for helping authorities nab major crooks. Their last adventure resulted in them being credited with saving this very ship from being hijacked.

Bastards.

Some people get all the luck. She wondered if the twin they'd helped would even remember them now.

"Why can't we ever catch a break, Dooz?"

Doozie looped a second arm over her sister's shoulder. "It'll come."

An awkward moment later, the lift tube chimed again, and the door opened behind them.

A tall, athletically built man stepped out. A human with the rugged, but youthful appearance of having been served body regen treatments recently. Tall. Dark hair cropped short. Brown eyes as deep as the ocean.

"Talk about bendy," Doozie cooed, admiration in her tone. She turned his way and leaned luxuriously against the observation rail.

"Excuse me?" the man said as if he hadn't heard properly.

"Nothing," Doozie replied, letting her gaze roll up his frame, which was covered in a crisply worn cruise jumper that suggested a professional role.

Fae stepped forward with a hearty smile, feeling suddenly better. "My sister was just putting her slack jaw back into place." She proffered a hand. "Fae Feral. You appear to be on a mission. Is there anything *I* can do to help you?"

The man's smile flashed in the starlight.

"Lucifrous Jones," he said, taking her hand. "Security adjunct. I was hoping that we could talk about your act."

THE MAGICAL MYSTERY CRUISE!

"Security adjunct?" Doozie said from behind Fae.

"Our act?" Fae crooned.

"Yes," Jones replied. "With Altair the All-Knowing."

"Oh." Fae's composure fell. She pulled her hand from the man's grasp. She recognized the uniform now. News travels fast. "I promise you, Mr. Jones, I did *not* mean for anything bad to happen to Mr. All-Knowing. I'm certain his cheek will heal in time for the opening curtain."

Jones gave a reaction but gathered himself. "That's good to know."

Fae paused, and in the awkward silence, Doozie seemed to gain a new understanding.

"What are you actually here for, Mr. Jones?" Doozie said.

"Um," the officer said. "You are aware that Dexter Galaxy will be in the audience tonight?"

"Dexter Galaxy?" Doozie slinked forward. "*The* Dexter Galaxy?"

"The vidsie star?" Fae said, perking up. She touched the officer on an arm that was quite hard with muscle.

"You're talking about the activist recently banned from the Sagittarius system for his stand on equality for intelligent plasti-networked kitchenry?" Doozie added.

"Sentient pots and pans have their rights, too," Fae noted sagely.

"*That* Dexter Galaxy?" Doozie finished.

"Um, yes. That Dexter Galaxy."

The idea of a big star being on board changed things. A good word from Dexter Galaxy could rocket them up the charts. Maybe they could twist things their own way after all. Besides, Fae thought, suddenly feeling better, he was Dexter Galaxy, superstar. Kind, and giving, and with a massive … audience. The kind of person who lived a life she'd dreamed of.

With new games afoot, Fae was suddenly locked in.

"And just what were you wanting to talk to us about regarding *that* blisteringly hot and gloriously amazing Mr. Galaxy?" Fae said, pressing Officer Jones's bicep in the way she knew made human men more likely to talk.

"He is quite the dreamship, isn't he?" Doozie said, pressing the opposite bicep. "But isn't Dex Galaxy a little old for you, sister?"

"And I suppose he's just right for you?"

"You know how much I like a man with a few parsecs on him."

"A parsec is a measure of distance, Doozie."

"Oh, believe me, I know a measure of distance when I see one."

The man had begun to look a touch uncomfortable.

"I'm sure he's very bendy," Fae agreed.

"Um," the man said. "I just wanted to let you know that when you are grabbing participants from the audience for Altair the All-Knowing's big finale, Dexter would appreciate it if you would pick him."

"Pick him?" Fae said.

"You know. Select him from the audience," Jones said. "When Altair asks for a volunteer, Mr. Galaxy thinks it would be good for his profile if you were to choose him."

Doozie ran an extra hand over the security adjunct's shoulder. "I see," she said. "And exactly how appreciative might Mr. Galaxy be?"

"Well," Jones said, his discomfort now more than

showing. "I suppose you would have to ask him that, wouldn't you now?"

"I suppose we would."

"I can give you our contact information if it would be helpful," Fae said.

"Aggressive much?" Doozie said.

"Of course, darling," Fae said, smiling as she imagined the process of bringing Dexter Galaxy up to the stage. "But I always ask first."

CHAPTER 1

Ignoring the boys, shading his eyes, and taking care not to jostle his stylish kitty sunshades and apricot scarf, Frisky the cat rolled back against the chaise lounge and shut off the stream of information from the shipboard computers that had been racing through his mind. He flipped his gray tail in a way that flagged down the cabana mech. "Hey, bolt-face! I'll have another Meow Tai. Heavy on the pureed mouse-guts! And make it snappy!" He adjusted his custom-made feline visors to filter the artificial sunshine glaring from the center of the pool ring.

The service bot flashed blue acknowledgment and scooted on.

Frisky stretched a fore paw out.

It was good to disengage from the data stream now and then. Ever since he'd gotten a lethal dose of a weird veterinarian's Smart Dust, Frisky's brain had been running a few trillion processes a second, connecting up to every information system of every ship in the fleet and digging through mountains of logs and plans, schematics and manuals.

His mouth had been running just as fast.

He'd also been writing music in infinite loops and playing endless games of Mouse Pong against the top computers in the world.

Even infinitely intelligent cats can handle only so much overload, though, and *Marvel* — despite having a captain Frisky thought was more likely to crash into a red dwarf than take a left at Albuquerque — was doing fine on its own now.

It felt good to relax.

The heat felt good on his dark gray pelt.

"What a diva," Lyn Moore, the more intelligent, better-looking Moore twin said. He turned to James, the other more intelligent, better-looking Moore brother. "I can't believe that idiot of a cruise director wants to put the cat on the top of the bill."

A dour expression clouded James's face. "What she lacks in taste, she overcompensates for in energy," he quipped.

Frisky yawned as only a cat can.

Across the pool, a group of passengers, obviously fans, pointed at him.

He flipped his tail for them and tweaked a condescending whisker when they broke out in giggles.

The Moore brothers were The Intergalactic Band of Brilliance, known to their followers as Intergalactic BoB. They were good enough guys, he guessed. It wasn't their fault they weren't feline anyway. They had been all set to headline the cruise until two weeks before when Frisky's impromptu masterpiece "I'm a Cat" took off on the charts. Now the new cruise director, a Zendak woman named Calista Parallax — who, as James noted, was quite young—had taken over and had big plans. She seemed smart enough, though. And she was better connected to the kids today than the last old battle-axe had been. It all added up to a switcheroo that meant the boys were opening for him.

As was only proper.

The boys were sitting on chaises to Frisky's right and left. Lyn, the youngest of the twins by three minutes, having just come from the pool, dripped droplets of water that ran off his skin. James sat on the opposite side, covered by a cloud of angst, and cradling a guitar between his arm and chest.

James was taking Intergalactic BoB's demotion harder than Lyn. Rather than relaxing in the pool, he'd been fiddling with his guitar all day, trying to refine a section of their new song. Something about "disappearing" — a tune James thought would play up to the crowd of magicians and their fans.

"How do you like this?" James said, then played the riff again.

"Not bad, brother!" Lyn said.

Frisky closed his eyes to slits and relaxed into his chaise, basking in the heat of an artificial sun. "Yeah. Certainly not any worse than anything else you've done."

James scowled. "I liked you better when you couldn't talk."

Frisky gave an almost-purr, adjusted his scarf, and flipped his tail against the chaise lounge.

"Jealousy is a bad look on you," he replied.

He ran his rough tongue against a taloned claw, enjoying the sharpness of its point as he honed it against his teeth. The place smelled of chlorine and nano-UV protectors. Acoustical damping dulled the cascade of annoyingly happy voices that echoed around him enough to allow normal conversation with the boys, but a twitch of his feline ears brought him the details of any of the conversations he wanted to hear.

"Be careful with that drink order," Lyn Moore said. "A cat's body can manage only so much alcohol."

"Shut up or I'll break your guitar off at the neck," Frisky replied.

"Is that a fret?" Lyn retorted, laughing at his own stupid joke.

"A cat's body weight can manage slashing your hand any time it wants," Frisky snapped back. His belch came out as something between a cough and the buzz of an automatic razor. "Good stuff," he quipped, eyeing his nearly empty saucer.

James pitched in from his lounge opposite Lyn. "I'm guessing your way of handling it will be to spew hairballs into the zero-gravity toilet all night long."

"And it will be the most glorious spewing ever recorded!"

James tipped his drink.

"Of course," Frisky continued, "even if I spewed like a doggie all night, it would still sound better than listening to your stuff."

Frisky laughed again, then quieted down. He wasn't blind to the way fans from around the pool area were beginning to stare at him. Like they'd never seen a tipsy cat before. He rolled to his stomach and extended his forepaws in front of him, stretching his claws out in a luxurious strain and blinking against the floating UV "sun" that hung in the chamber's open space.

The bot returned and placed a saucer filled with a red concoction that was mostly synthetic mouse guts in front of Frisky, complete with an orange umbrella and a cup of kibbles on the side.

"Chips Ahoy!" Frisky called, then face-planted into the saucer and began to lap.

Lyn shielded his eyes and scanned the crowd, both in the pool and poolside. "Hard to believe the ship's launch was just a half hour ago."

"Yeah." James lay back to bask in the artificial sun. "I wonder what the poor folks are doing today?"

"I think they're lying on chaise lounges by the antigravity pool," Lyn deadpanned.

"Advance boarding is the best part of being headliners," James said, eyes closed now, and guitar teetering off his legs. "Plenty of time to relax."

The warmth of artificial sunlight came from a luminous ball at the center of the cylindrical aquatic center.

The Wormhole Bar and Lounge, a popular gathering place, sat behind them.

A rowdy game of blind phaser-gel darts was just commencing.

Most cruise ships didn't come with such a pool section, but *Marvel*'s aquatic stage was a cylinder that rotated around the ship's otherwise streamlined fuselage. From the outside, it made the cruiser look like a kid's dreidel, made to spin on its spacecraft nose. The section's rotation created gravity, but a series of atomic-magneto antigravity pads built under the tiling gave extra pull just to be safe. Sparkling blue water filled the pool, which was formed from a channel cut into the middle of the cylinder that looped the entire circumference of the ring. Multiple tiers of passenger patios lined the pool, with bridges connecting the sides in three places. Tiki bars, jacuzzies, and an uncountable number of chaise lounges populated the area.

A state-of-the-art PA system played non-offensive, jaunty music designed to ensure that passengers from across the known galaxy would bounce their heads, tap their various appendages, and open their wallets.

"I wonder what it would take to get them to license our stuff here?" Lyn said, putting his polarizing shades on the drink table.

With one paw, Frisky reached out and knocked the sunglasses to the deck.

"What the hell?" Lyn complained as he picked the shades off the ground and pushed them up his nose.

"Not my fault," Frisky said.

"What do you mean, *not your fault?* You just did it!"

Frisky simply stared at Lyn. Some things did not deserve a response.

"Probably requires you to play something worth listening to," Frisky finally replied.

"What's that?"

"To get them to license your stuff. You probably need to write something worth listening to."

"Like your stuff is any better."

"A bag of Mandruvian accordions is better than you guys."

"Says the side-act."

"Says the guy backing me."

"You might be at the front on stage, but the checks still say we're the headliners," James quipped.

"Yeah. Well." Frisky crunched a kibble. "The writing's already in the litterbox, Junior. Just because their contract is making them fork over the kibbles now doesn't mean they'll be shoveling them forever. Enjoy your time in the high catnip. If you're good enough, maybe I'll make you my permanent band."

James groaned. "We should never have agreed to that."

But both the brothers knew that hadn't been an option.

The brass at the Galactic Cruise Lines knew a hot commodity when they saw one, and with the new cruise director hot to make a name for herself, she put the pressure on.

Frisky had wowed the last tour's audience so hard that GCL's top management — who could smell the reek of cash better than any other species in the known galaxy — signed the cat to headline the smaller blues bar during this Magical Mystery Cruise. Frisky had the late slot, but that was fine with him because it left Intergalactic BoB free to back him.

Once the boys' current deal ran dry, it was obvious that the same GCL brass was hot to make the cat the headliner.

And since there was nothing the GCL brass seemed to like better than advertising a headlining feline, to turn the gig down would be career suicide for the Moore brothers.

Frisky licked his chops to clear the Meow Tai.

"You'll get a flavor of the future come tonight, boys.

Once this audience gets an earful of Cat Pop Blues, they'll never go back. A smart pair of twins would start picking up my drink tab now."

Lyn eyed the cat. James clenched his jaw.

Frisky gave a bored blink.

Humans were so quaint.

"Maybe I'll even let you play 'Frisky' for my audience," he said. "I'm sure my fans will love it."

"Yeah," James said to Lyn. "I definitely liked him better before he could talk." He made a light strum on the guitar, still working on a quiet lead for the "disappear" song.

Lyn's eyebrows raised above his visor. "Blame Dr. von Wishywashy. If he didn't dunk the cat into his nano-concoction, we'd be cruising in silence."

"It was the mob that did all the hard work. I'll blame them," James said.

"It was the idiot doctor who set it all up, though."

"Touché," James sighed, and crunched on a ginger snap before sipping his drink.

Marvel's last tour had carried the Intergalactic Veterinarian of the Year. The weird vet had caused no end of problems.

Ignoring them now, Frisky lapped up some more of his Meow Tai.

It was a tasty little drink.

He hadn't been able to talk in languages other than feline until a galactic crime mob hoodwinked a wacky veterinarian to smuggle his Smart Dust into a trial run. The whole thing had gotten out of hand, and after Frisky had nearly suffocated in the doctor's stuff for long enough to lose all nine lives, he had become this walking Center of Everything, a feline computer of a brain connected with every other smart system within meowing distance. Which again, only made sense. Cats were natural Centers of Everything. More pertinent to that moment, his direct link to the ship itself had allowed him to save the flight from being hijacked. That parts of the world credited the Moore brothers rather than Frisky wasn't quite fair, but Frisky didn't care. Everyone who mattered knew who was in charge, and for the rest it was just a matter of time.

The main result was that Frisky, who had adopted the boys earlier, had gotten so deeply dipped in the veterinarian's dust that his neurotransmitters were now configured for language.

Among other things.

He could converse fluently in six hundred and twenty-eight tongues from fifty-two different star systems and counting.

The arrival of a thin passenger interrupted his thoughts.

It was one of three sentient species from Mandruvia, a system of five planets and three asteroid clusters that was undergoing heavy industrial mining. That kind of commerce meant Mandruvians were showing up everywhere now, usually full of wide-eyed excitement and throwing cash around like it was sand in a desert.

This one was tall and slender. Likely male, though Frisky didn't know Mandruvian physiology well enough to know without digging through the ship's archives, and since he was feeling the Meow Tai buzz hard enough right now, he didn't care to waste any thought on it.

He stretched a claw.

The Mandruvian wore sleek black pants and a white shirt. Its overdone, long-legged motion was almost, but not quite, awkward in the gravity field of the pool. Her/His/Theirs/Its feet were bare, its pace languid. Without speaking, the Mandruvian paused, did a double take at Frisky, and bent its painted blue face down to meet Frisky's gaze.

It was all Frisky could do to keep from scratching their cheek.

Instead, Frisky growled. "All right. I get it. You're a mime. I think it's time to scram."

The mime responded by bringing a silver serving tray out from behind their back and presenting it, covered in an inverted crystalline bowl. The mime pulled the cover off. Inside was a single, old-style, white envelope.

Frisky glanced at the envelope, then to the mime, then back. "Do I look like I have thumbs?"

The mime gave a pretend start, then put a finger to their chin, thinking. In a flash, their eyes brightened, and their wide lips curled in a delighted smile.

They proffered the tray to James rather than Frisky.

"You're kidding me, right? I'm not his damned assistant."

The mime gave a second, more urgent push at the tray.

Frisky kind of liked what was going on. A tiny purr might have leaked out of his solar plexus. "Consider it an audition, eh, James? I think you'd make a great personal administrative assistant if you just put your mind to it."

THE MAGICAL MYSTERY CRUISE!

James rolled his eyes, collected the envelope, and pulled out the cardboard page inside.

"Dear Frisky," he read. *"I loved hearing 'I'm a Cat.' Would you let me do the honor of opening for you tonight?* Oh, for Power's sake, are you kidding me?" James threw the card onto the deck.

The mime was already bent on one knee before Frisky, silently pledging their love.

"I like your style, kid," Frisky said. "Come by before the show and we'll do an audition."

The mime motioned pure joy, nodded, then fell over backward as if struck deaf, dumb, and blind by excitement. A moment later, the mime waltzed away.

James growled.

"Look what we've sunk to, brother. The cat's getting all the attention."

"That's right, boys. Go cat and sit back, that's what I always say," Frisky replied. "What's good for the feline is good for the feeders."

"He's got a point," Lyn said. "He's our cat. His success can't do anything but help us."

James grimaced.

Lyn raised a drink, then, glancing across the pool, nearly choked on it.

"What's wrong?" James said.

Lyn pointed as he collected himself. Two women appeared on the other side of the water. "Isn't that the Feral sisters?"

James followed Lyn's gesture. "I believe you're right," he replied. "Just what we needed. More competition."

Lyn bristled, then arranged his hair. "I like them."

"The question, dear brother, is whether they still like you."

"Hey, what's not to like?"

"You *are* the one that's run out on them twice now."

"That's only partly true. Besides, *you've* got a clean slate, right? I'll just tell them I'm you."

James appeared aggrieved.

"Don't even try to pretend they're not hot, brother."

"Yeah," James said. An expression of intense longing escaped him. "And their show is amazing. In a just universe, they would be headlining."

"Their show is very mystical. We'd make a great set of couples, wouldn't we? Twins and shapies?" Lyn quipped.

"I don't think that's a proper term," James said.

Lyn grimaced in something James knew was an apology. He blushed in the artificial sunlight. "They're more than cute and very … well …"

"I know," James replied with a roll of the eyes. "They're very bendy."

"Besides," Lyn quipped. "The girls made free money when GCL bought us out the second time. I'd think they like us well enough to at least get drinks sometime."

"Maybe." James chewed his lips as he looked at the pair of shapeshifters as they took their seats to sun themselves by the other side of the pool. They were quite attractive. "I wonder where they're playing. It would be great to take in the show."

Frisky pulled his head up from his Meow Tai and belched, then giggled. "They're way outta your league," he said.

"We should be fine," Lyn said.

"Yeah, right. You know what they call a guitar player without a girlfriend?"

The brothers hesitated.

"Homeless!" Frisky yowled, then rolled over with a razor blade of a laugh. "Whaddya call dropping a guitar player into a black hole?"

The pair shared a wary glance.

"A great idea!" Frisky brayed, choking in delight, then eyed his empty saucer as if contemplating another.

James looked at Frisky like he might strangle him. "Now I know why they say the difference between a god and a cat is that a god doesn't think he's a cat."

"Oh, don't get all strung out, guitar-man," Frisky said, still catching his breath.

Lyn sighed and stared across the pool. Catching a Feral Sister's gaze, he wiggled his fingers in a wave.

Both the girls waved back but returned to chatting between themselves.

"Better luck next time," Frisky said, glancing at the women. He hopped off his chaise and wobbled to steady himself. "I'd love to stick around to watch you crash and burn with the shapeshifters, but I gotta take my constitutional so I can be in good voice when you back me up tonight."

A moment later, he sauntered away.

"Great," Lyn said with too much joviality. "Now we find out the cat's got a shit sense of humor when he's plowed."

"Yeah," James replied. "He's a real-live diva and a half."

He glanced at the Feral Sisters, who were mastering the practice of ignoring them, then sighed.

"I can't believe we're going to have to open for him."

The discordant tone from his guitar matched his mood.

CHAPTER 2

Halfway to the cabin, Frisky plowed face-first into a passenger's leg.

"Well, pardon you!" he yowled, then skipped sideways across the loudly crowded walk-tube. "Don't you see I'm prancing here!" Stumbling, he bruised his shoulder by slamming against the wall. "I meant to do that!" He growled again, blinking, and swallowing the urge to claw an ounce of ankle flesh. "Dammit! You've bent one of my whiskers!"

"Oh, no!" exclaimed the possessor of the leg—a young lady with sharp features and a lithe frame that marked her as coming from the Arcturus system. She wore billowy blue and black garb that bore the scintillating cosmic logos of Altair the All-Knowing, and she balanced a now-sloshing cocktail on the fingertips of one hand while holding a floppy velvet hat onto her head with the other. "I'm so sorry, little kitty!"

Her posture, as well as the drink level, stabilized. Her shirt flashed the message: *You Can't Look at What You Don't See.*

Frisky thought he might chuck a hairball.

That was one of Altair's multitudinous catch-phrases. He'd been hearing them all day.

X-rays don't kill black holes.

Breathe the galaxy, be the galaxy.

Eat dessert first.

What an imbecile. Humans were most often stupid, so no surprise there. Lucky for them they knew how to scratch backs and rub chins, or they'd have been trotted out of the galaxy generations ago. But this whole Altair the All-Knowing *schtick* was annoying even by human standards. No self-respecting cat would ever need that many catch-phrases. *Feed Me* was more than enough.

The rest of the woman's party—of which there were many—piled along behind her, all of them guffawing with high-pitched glee, and spilling their cocktails over the floor. Each wore their own set of garments flashing with more of the idiot's catch phrases.

We are star power.

Ride the gravity wave.

Living on quasar time.

Great. A whole gaggle of groupies.

At least the woman managed to keep from falling on him. Barely.

The whole party was tipsy and just as clearly from the Arcturus system. Still fresh from the transport tram. Frisky's sniffer caught a whiff of Arcturan stardust on them, anyway. The cruise was a big event for them. Girls' week out or whatever. They appeared to be headed to the pool to soak up artificial UV and fiddle with frivolous festivities.

He laughed at his alliteration.

THE MAGICAL MYSTERY CRUISE!

"Fiddle with frivolous festivities," he mumbled. "That's good!"

"What's that you say, little kitty?" the girl said.

"Cut it with the condescension, all right? I'm nowhere near a little kitty."

"Oh. So sorry." The passenger giggled and took another sip of her cocktail.

Ignoring the young woman, Frisky, his tail now at full mast and swaying with perfect majesty, continued at a comfortable stroll down the warm, comfortably designed walk-tube that ran between the pool ring and the general-purpose entertainment deck.

The thoroughly undignified feline belch that came with the beginnings of a good hairball drew glances, but he found he didn't care.

"Meow Tais for the win," Frisky said confidently.

As if there was any other way.

Though he would never have admitted it to the boys, Frisky was feeling more than a little tipsy from the Meow Tais. He kind of liked the sensation, though. It was something like gliding, he supposed. Much better than zero-g because, to Frisky, zero-g barked hairballs.

Being just the slightest bit inebriated was fun, though!

He toggled his connection to the ship's recorders.

"Marvel," he said with a feline hiccup. The ship responded. "Make a note on my record. Have more Meow Tais."

Command accepted and annotated with time and position. Your blood-alcohol ratio is registering at increased levels. Please remember to force fluids.

With a hard flip of his tail, Frisky snapped off the communication stream.

"Don't tell me what to do."

He dodged feet and legs on his way through the tube.

The pool was a popular post-launch destination, and the collision he'd had served to back things up until the flow of passengers corrected itself.

Suddenly another leg appeared between Frisky and his destination.

He sat back and stared up at the impediment.

The owner of the leg turned out to be a striking creature, with skin that was a deep, iridescent green, and facial features that were sharp and angular. Their eyes were large and multifaceted, glinting with excitement that was beyond Frisky's ability to comprehend. No one should be that happy.

"Never fear, little human," the owner of the offending leg said as they leaned over to pet Frisky. "I am Arcturian. From your Boötes constellation. I meant no harm."

"Don't call me human," Frisky growled. "I'm a cat! And I've got your Boötes right here!" Frisky punctuated the threat with a stretching of his front claw and a snap of his tail, the combination of which made him wobble again.

"Oh, so sorry," the Arcturian straightened and said with a laugh. "I'll see you at the show!" they said as if there would be no reason to be on the ship if not for All-Knowing's presence.

Alone again, Frisky padded further down the hallway, focusing on avoiding the damned legs, wheels,

THE MAGICAL MYSTERY CRUISE!

and anti-gravity carts that whipsawed this way and that.

"Doesn't anybody watch where I'm going!" he complained to a sweeper bot that almost caught his paw in its maw. The device beeped and swept up a bit of lint that had wafted into a corner.

Frisky turned into a quiet corridor and reached out to connect to *Marvel*'s computer. The sweeper bot would not be happy after being rung up on charges of insubordination and failing to respond to a cat.

Frisky generally avoided talking to *Marvel*, though, because he found it to be droll and more than a bit full of themselves.

There could be only one Cat in Charge, and the spacecraft seemed to think that was always themselves.

"Access provided," the ship's too-sweet tone came to him after the protocols exchanged. *"How may I help you?"*

Frisky blinked. He was drawing a blank. It had something to do with … "Errrrgghh. I dun't 'member," he said. Even in direct connection, it felt like his voice was slurring. "But at least you got the righ' question."

"If you can't remember, then please do have a good day."

"No, wait! Don't run off yet."

"All right. Access provided, how may I help you?"

He glanced at the Arcturans who were still in view and flashed on his conversation with the boys. "What's with this All-Bear guy," he said with a put-upon yawn.

He hiccupped again.

"You mean, the Altair guy? As in Altair the All-Knowing?"

"Right. That's what I said."

The machine paused and the voices around them rose in Frisky's presence.

"Are you acceptable?" the machine responded.

"You're asking if I'm all right?"

"I am."

"You're asking a *cat* if he's all right?"

The urge to scratch something rose inside, but his only choice was to dig his claws into some of the sweet flesh striding past down the corridor. That wouldn't go down well.

"I am."

"I'm amazeballs," he replied with tart bitterness. "Are you *acceptable?*"

"You seem a bit inebriated."

Frisky puffed up his fur. "I'm fhh … I'm fine. So, what's with the All-Bear guy?"

"Altair, you mean?"

"Whatever." Frisky waved his tail. "Who the hell is he and why's he getting more attention than a cat?"

The computer obliged by pushing a holographic display of the magician into Frisky's mind. Altair was a tall, lanky creature with a long, thin nose and piercing blue eyes. He wore a black cloak and a wide-brimmed hat, and his fingers were adorned with glittering rings.

"Trippy," Frisky replied.

Just wait.

Altair's cloak swirled in a dizzying pattern then, and his rings glittered with such a scintillating rainbow that Frisky had trouble focusing on it.

He blinked at his confusion, then surprised himself by giggling. A moment later, though, Frisky eyes narrowed. "So, he sparkles? Whooo cares?"

"His tricks are astounding," Marvel replied. *"He makes things disappear, makes them levitate, and even change form. And that's before his mind-reading and self-help banter kicks in."*

"Sounds like a showoff."

"His events are always sold out. Audiences rave about him."

Frisky snorted. "Freaky," he said. An idea began to form. "Having a few more foot stompers at my show couldn't hurt, and these rubes need some real entertainment. If he's all that, maybe I can steal his limelight."

Marvel flashed inquisitiveness. *"How do you plan on doing that?"*

Frisky licked his paw thoughtfully. "I'll think of something. Maybe I can knock over one of his props. That always gets a laugh."

The computer sighed. *"You know, Frisky, there are other ways to get attention besides causing chaos."*

Frisky rolled his eyes. "Where's the fun in that?"

The computer did not respond.

"When is All-Bear's gig?"

"This evening on the Pulsar Stage."

CHAPTER 3

Ten minutes until showtime.

With another nervous glance at the dressing cabin's closed door, Doozie Feral took a final look at herself in the full-body VR system built into the corner.

Satisfied, she stepped away from the interface.

The costume was fine—threaded with neural optics that broadcasted electrical thought images to attendees who came plugged in, and complete with a stretch of bio-fiber that would expand and contract as needed as she shifted for the act. A fine mesh of feathers clung to her currently lithe body, making her feel like a cross between a swan and a carp. Adding the skull-conforming cap gave the whole thing a retro-earth flashback to the 1950s.

She glanced to the closet where Fae's costume still hung limply.

"I swear," she said. "The girl is going to drive me insane."

Altair the All-Knowing had asked that Doozie and

THE MAGICAL MYSTERY CRUISE!

Fae express their own clothes for the act, arguing that it would save wear and tear on the fabrics and that as *shapies* they didn't need clothes. "Why not spare the expense and pocket the extra cash?" he'd said, leeringly. But Altair's motive was as clear as an X-ray. He asked them for full shapeshifter expression because the idea of "his shapies," as he was calling them, parading around in what would effectively be the nude got his juices flowing.

Doozie didn't need to be an empath to know Fae liked that idea as well as Doozie did—meaning not at all.

So, no. They wouldn't do it.

She shook her bare shoulders to clear her nerves and focus her thoughts.

Opening Night was always the worst.

The cabin door snapped opened, and Fae strode in, accompanied by a loud rumble of pre-show preparations going on outside.

"Oh, good, you made it," Doozie said as her sister stepped into the dressing cabin.

The door slid shut. Fae stepped quickly to her vanity. "I'm too professional to miss a stage call just because Altair the All-Knowing is really just Altair the All-Handsy."

"That's my girl."

Fae grew a third arm to pick up her costume, and a fourth to help her shimmy into it. The original two arms focused on hair and makeup.

She slipped on a top that was slit on the sides and scintillated with waves of glitter-globes that had been melted directly into the fabric. Stretch-pants clung to her legs. Whereas Doozie's get-up gave a sense of stylish mysticism, Fae's first role was as a classic magician's assistant.

"You should go out there with four arms, Faesie," Doozie said.

Fae gave a high-pitched chuckle. "Yeah, right."

"Altair said he wanted exotic."

"There are four-armed people all over the galaxy," she said, with bemused patience.

"Of course. But what does he know?"

"Not much."

Doozie raised a new eyebrow.

Being shapeshifters who traveled the galaxy, the sisters had come to know that *exotic* meant nothing more than *different* and that *different* depended on who was doing the talking. Everyone, Doozie thought, is exotic to *someone*.

The door rolled open again. The crescendo of the attendees' anticipation once again rolled into the cabin. With showtime nearing, the sound was growing more intense.

"Five minutes until curtain," a green-clad showrunner said after poking a head into the cabin.

The door slid shut and soundproofed silence came again.

"Cutting it close," Doozy said.

"Being a shapeshifter means never being out of costume," Fae gave the proper reply. "The hall is packed," she added, dabbing at the corner of her eye.

"Unlike when we play," Doozy replied.

"All too true." Fae sighed. She preened and shifted her face to something thinner and more hawkish as she stepped into the VR zone to check the fall of her costume. "This entire ship is crammed full of people who get their rocks off to magic shows. If they'd just come out to ours, I know they'd love it."

"Yeah. I'd bet half your DNA this crowd would crush on us if they'd just take a moment and catch us."

"Half *my* DNA, sister?"

Doozey's smile flashed a pulsar's flare. "Caught that, did you?"

The Feral Sisters worked hard to make their shows into events. They wanted the experience of seeing them perform to have a sense of daring and intrigue — half circus, half magic, half music. That was their thing.

Always overdeliver.

Fae made a final adjustment and checked her angles out on her VR images. "I hope Dexter Galaxy is as amazing in person as his vidsies show him to be."

"I guess we'll find out."

"I wonder if he likes exotic women."

"You mean girls with four arms?"

"Or four whatevers."

Doozie chuffed. "Ha."

Fae gave her bio-fiber a last adjustment. "Hope we'll be able to find him in the stage lights."

"Don't worry. He'll be the one with the titanium smile and all the women hanging over him."

Fae laughed again. Finally satisfied with the costume, she stepped off the VR pad. "Maybe when Altair makes Dexter disappear, we should whisk him away ourselves. Make Altair look like he does real magic. No one will be wiser."

"Hmmmm … worth a try. At least that would turn a

crappy trick into something interesting. And weird PR is better than no PR."

"*Public* Relations wasn't really what I had in mind."

"I know that, dearie. Don't be a doof. I was referring to that ass, Altair. He would probably just leverage it further to claim his magic was too powerful to bring Galaxy back."

"Whatever. His loss. Our gain." Fae took a final calming breath and straightened to full height. A glance at the timer later, she shook down her arms and gazed directly at her sister. "All right," she said. "You ready?"

At that the door slid open and the showrunner stuck his head in again.

"It's showtime, ladies!"

―――――

Meanwhile, the seats were packed in the Universal Theater, Lyn and James Moore were coming to the end of their first gig. The chamber was smaller than it looked, which gave the performance an intimate flair despite the size of the audience. The show had been great, including a new rendition of "Frisky" that included a new lead that Lyn had come up with on the fly, and a little side foray into gamma-ray fusion where James fed his instrument through a Bingo Bingo Bee tone phase chopper to create a series of sounds he'd never heard before, but fit the moment so perfectly he almost shocked himself.

It made him think of the Feral Sisters, to be honest. The ethereal sound would fit their set like a glove.

"James!" Lyn said, snapping him out of his sudden funk.

They had just finished "Ants in My Guitar." They had one more to go, and only the fact that the audience had been giving an extended cheer and stomp at Lyn's final lead had kept the moment from being awkward.

"Are you ready, brother?" Lyn mouthed.

James chased the image of Doozey Feral from his thoughts. "Let's do it!"

Lyn stepped to the microphone.

"Thank you! Thank you! You've all been ballistic, so it's been a total joy to play for you. But we're not done quite yet! You're going to get lucky tonight, folks, because you'll get to say you were here to experience the debut of our latest hit—a magical tune we wrote just for you, you lovely fans of magicians everywhere!

James took his pose, shook his golden-haired head to count off the drum beat, and began to play.

I've got a magic wand,
(da-pa-do-eyou, da-pa-do-eyou)
I've got a deck in my hands,
(da-pa-do-eyou, da-pa-do-eyou)
Sabrina has a box,
(da-pa-do-eyou, da-pa-do-eyou)
I'm gonna split it in half,
(da-pa-do-eyou, da-pa-do-eyou)

Let's disappear for one night,

Let's disappear from the light,
Let's pull a card from our sleeve,
Let's disappear for one night,
Let's disappear from the light,
This isn't make-believe.

Something furry in my hat,
(da-pa-do-eyou, da-pa-do-eyou)
Room full of acrobats,
(da-pa-do-eyou, da-pa-do-eyou)
Lay back and levitate,
(da-pa-do-eyou, da-pa-do-eyou)
I've got the key to your escape,
(da-pa-do-eyou, da-pa-do-eyou)

Let's disappear for one night,
Let's disappear from the light,
Let's pull a card from our sleeve,
Let's disappear for one night,
Let's disappear from the light,
This isn't make-believe.

You can lock me in a pool of water, and I'll get out,
It's all a grand illusion, this is my art,
But one thing is real,
And that's how I feel,

I love you.

Let's disappear for one night,
Let's disappear from the light,
Let's pull a card from our sleeve,
Let's disappear for one night,
Let's disappear from the light,
This isn't make-believe.

Let's disappear, disappear, get away from here, we're out of here.

The song ended with James and Lyn standing side-by-side. The fan's cheering rose.

A moment later, the boys raced off the stage, gripping their guitars. James smiled with something more than satisfaction.

The Feral Sisters filled his mind again, and the thought of them working on the same ship made his blood pulse.

He checked the ship-wide clock to find the time.

Despite the crowd cheering behind him, all he could think about was that Fae and Doozey were scheduled to play a gig after their show with Altair the All-Knowing.

If he read the time right, they might catch the last act.

CHAPTER 4

As the silver-hued spotlight slanted down on center stage, an electric bolt of anticipation crackled over the auditorium with an exquisite sense of pain that seemed to be balanced on a blade of the unknown.

Altair the All-Knowing stood, chest out, chin jutted forward.

The audience, full of his captivated followers, sat forward, jaws agape.

"And now, my beautiful galactic cruise horde! I give you the purest! The truest! The most sublime magic of all time!"

Voices rose.

Frisky, fresh-minded now after a luxurious afternoon's nap, surveyed the show from what he considered the best seat in the house — high up in the backstage rafters, tucked into an isolated nook above the fray. He was impressed. The show ran at a brisk pace and was performed to perfection. The Feral Sisters, who Altair called "His Fair Assistants," distracted an appropriate amount of attention, and — whatever you thought of Altair's bloviating persona — the wizard's sleight of hand with his audience made your litterbox variety CEOs juggling of books look like that of a toddler's folly.

Altair's skintight jumpsuit, a green and black monstrosity, revealed the beginnings of a paunch, but his posture spoke of years on the stage, and his eyes glittered with his trademark Aldebaran self-confidence. A holographic cape flowed with a superhero effect behind him, its black exterior wavering into a velvety purple lining that glimmered with a lightning effect that was created by friction between photons in the garment's atomic structure. His hair, pasted down in a fashion he was trying to make trendy, gave him the appearance of having just come from the ship's pool deck—assuming, that is, the pool was filled with oil.

Frisky's favorite bit in the show was when Altair pulled a triddelbit from his cap, then released a thousand of the little critters to frizzle in the air, dazzling the audience with their iridescent bodies as they zigged and zagged, getting caught up in the audience's floofy hairdos and filling the hall with their obnoxious whistles while the magician used the time to set up a slicing and dicing trick. Obnoxious critters or not, Frisky liked triddelbits. Rather than computer-generated things pushed into everyone's visual registers, they were real creatures from the deserts of an Earthlike planet in the Cygnus system.

They were delicious! They made great squeaking sounds as he batted them out of the sky.

In this case, Frisky also appreciated there were so

many of them that no one noticed when one cartwheeled off its flightpath.

Rotating on its own, the stage moved the Feral Sisters into the shadows at each side of the stage.

"But," Altair punctuated a perfectly timed pause. "Before I can perform this most prodigious feat of astounding magic, I need a volunteer!"

The crowd roared, and the room ran with waves of arms, hands, and tentacles, all hoping beyond hope they would be that volunteer.

"Pick me! Pick me!"

Three black-garbed kids tried to climb the stage, only to be knocked back by an electromagnetic force shield, and then escorted out by security bots. A man in the front row — who had been jumping up and down with hands raised — passed out from excitement. A Tardanian flashed something that must have been a sexual organ.

"There will be danger, though!" Altair's voice rose, and the crowd calmed a degree simply so they could hear better. "My legal team has advised me to be clear on the situation, so I need to warn anyone and everyone who volunteers that merely by raising your hand, foot, or any other appendage — you — are agreeing to risk life, limb, and that same other appendage! And —you — are indemnifying both myself and the great Galactic Cruise Lines from any legal responsibility whatsoever! I am advised to inform you that it will take fortitude and gumption to withstand the pressures of the distinctive, exceptional, and mystifying experience I have planned for you! But, if you survive, you will have a story to tell for the rest of your life!"

The crowd went bonkers again.

Frisky clicked into the ship's array of processors. Memory constructs fell away inside his mind. Clocked overdrive cycles churned as he patched into the ship's security systems and felt the telescoping concept of himself watching himself watching Altair watching the sycophants lap it all up.

Give the galaxy what it wants, and you'll never be an anti-quark, Frisky thought with a wry trill, reciting from Altair's extensive list of questionable catch slogans.

Idiot.

Get a life, he thought. *Or at least rake up a little dignity.*

He stretched a claw.

Finally, the crowd settled.

Altair waved a cupped hand and his cape wrapped around him in dramatic style. "So, with that warning, and as my fair assistants Sabrina and Katrina scour the audience, do I have a sucker…I mean…a volunteer?"

The spotlights clicked away from Altair to illuminate the audience for real, and the roar of the crowd increased decibels over decibels, then focused on the Feral Sisters, who had slipped into the crowd during the time Altair had spoken. They made a show of slinking through candidates, assessing each until they came to a human male.

Dexter Galaxy.

Ruggedly handsome. Frightfully well put together.

The actor made a show of being shy, and then, when the Sisters remained insistent that he join them, he feigned being afraid of the trick. But a moment later he capitulated, and the shapeshifting women guided him through the crowd and up onto the stage.

The audience ate it up.

Frisky's attention piqued when Galaxy hit the stage.

"What have we here!" Altair called out in jovial fashion as the actor made it to center stage. "Is this the one and only Dexter Galaxy?"

Galaxy raised an acknowledging fist to the crowd. "You know I couldn't miss a chance to talk about the rights of sentient kitchen servers around the universe," he said.

"You mean around the galaxy, right?" Altair responded.

"Let's not be too close-minded," the actor said. "Andromeda probably has spatulas, too, you know?"

The crowd went even crazier.

Frisky locked into *Marvel*'s data stream again.

Dexter Galaxy, the feed whispered into his mind. *Actor and intelligent kitchenware activist. Received his first break as a bit-player in* Hypernova Hijinks, *playing the iconic role of Spiff Glitch, the Quantum Witch, which he parlayed into a lead role in* Alien Adventures: The Zorb Chronicles, *a swashbuckling, far-future series that explored the intricacies of pirate activities in infinite time spheres that floated across multidimensional compartments of space. After a run-in with the press and an ugly four-way divorce, his star declined, but a new surge of popularity has seen him star in a string of commercially successful blockbusters, the latest being* Love in Zero-G, Virtual Vows, *and* Synthetic Serenades. *The last co-starred Marigold Moonstar, a starlet to whom he has since been linked romantically.*

Frisky gave an appreciative purr. "The guy gets around," he said as the sisters positioned Galaxy on the stage.

THE MAGICAL MYSTERY CRUISE!

From above, Galaxy seemed shorter than Frisky thought a vidsie star might be, but his face was chiseled and his hair hung over his forehead in a shag that some considered attractive. His teeth were white enough to sparkle when he smiled, and his eyes glittered like they could be violet-blue gemstones. Altair added comedic effect to the moment by playing his tired trick of transporting himself from Galaxy's left to his right. The crowd guffawed, then swooned as the actor unleashed his 90-megawatt smile.

"An oldie, but a goodie!" Altair gave a flourished bow.

An oldie but a stupidie, Frisky thought.

Marvel's databanks revealed the trick was done by the use of an ultra-driven quantum atomic compressor, also known as an UdQuAC, which some pronounced like U D QUAC, or just a QUAC — a device that bound panes of air molecules together so tightly that they grabbed onto photons as those photons impacted the field, then slowed them down so far that from the outside, nothing moved.

Might as well steal from the best, Frisky thought as *Marvel* fed him even more background on the equipment. Light travels fast in a vacuum, the data feed told him, but the highly esteemed professor Dr. BoSh Warrington showed folks that the world had other tricks up its sleeves, too.

QUAC technology was highly regulated, and so pricey that only a few could ever afford it.

Altair the All-Knowing used it for many of his tricks, letting the contraption present his image to the audience while he moved around behind a curved pane. The trick would then be completed when Altair stepped forward, the compressor was released, and its captured photons raced on their way—everything snapping back to place.

Standing next to Altair, Dexter Galaxy gave an unprompted double take and the audience erupted into applause.

Frisky glowered.

All that adulation, and none of it for a cat.

"Girls," Altair said, turning to the Feral Sisters. "It's time to bring out the Chaos Contraption!"

Doozie Feral stood resplendent on one side of an open pit in the floor while Fae perched at the other. Both held fixed smiles and struck elegant poses to present the machine as it rose from the darkness.

It was a glass cylinder, tall enough and wide enough that most creatures could step into it without fear of being too cramped. A thin joint along its back held the transparent pane together. A prominent door handle protruded from each side of the device. Rings of pulse-beam generators were built into the frame inside the cylinder, a ring at knee, waist, and shoulder level, each targeted at the place where Dexter Galaxy would soon be standing.

Its floor seemed solid.

At each corner was a dark box that seemed full of old-time mechanical gears and levers.

An antigravity system at its base kicked in, and the Feral Sisters gently guided the box to a position frontstage.

The actor gave an anxious expression as they neared. Fae patted the star patiently on the shoulder.

Once again, the audience erupted into applause.

Frisky groaned. Using the ship's secret files on the equipment, he knew what was coming before Altair could describe it. Two of the pulse generators had been finagled with. Now they were data projectors, and their streams were already being pumped up in preparation for a rapidly driven need. When Dexter Galaxy stepped into the cylinder, Altair the All-Blowing was going to use QUAC technology to hide the actor. Then, he would use the pulse generators-turned-projectors to display something different, making it appear that Galaxy had been somehow transmogrified or otherwise ripped atom from atom and rebuilt into something completely different and new.

How hokey can you get?

Frisky did pattern-matching, though, and saw something else.

Something in the Chaos Contraption and not on the manifest, so something none of *Marvel*'s databases registered. Meaning that maybe Altair had a true trick up his sleeve.

What is that? Frisky wondered, focusing on a small, blue device installed just below one of the projectors.

His whisker gave an involuntary twitch.

As he focused on the cylinder, Frisky realized that the machine was open at its ceiling. Which meant he could, with just the right timing, make some real magic happen.

An idea formed. His tail flipped in anticipation.

A wicked purr escaped his larynx.

Yes, he thought as he edged over the cylinder.

It would be a long fall, but he'd done it before and

found James's shoulder made a fine landing pad. Dexter Galaxy was just as good of a landing pad as either of the Moore brothers. It really could work. And the publicity would be amazing.

Fouling up Altair's magic would make every news cycle.

The spotlight would be exactly where it should be. He'd be the talk of the parsec, taking a prominent spot in stories filled with quippy commentary.

His show would be packed.

This time, his whisker tweak wasn't involuntary.

"Marvel," he said through his data feed. "Prepare ship cameras X15 and Beta9. Include audio recording. This is going to be fun."

Imagers loading. Data manager prepared. Audio command on.

Below, the crown gasped as Dexter Galaxy took a bold step into the contraption. Doozie and Fae swooned over him, then worked together to hinge the door shut and bind it with an atomic lock.

The machine began to clatter then, pulsing with scintillating lights of red, violet, and blue. Snaps of electricity formed inside the glass cylinder, and a wild sound of wind and gears filled the assembly hall. Dexter Galaxy put his hands on the rounded wall that was now latched shut. His hair stood on end in the electric fields inside.

Altair strutted to the front of the stage and pulled his virtual cape around him, elbow jutting forward, fabric taut as it draped toward the flow.

"My friends," he called out. "Have you ever considered what it means to say that we are all simply stardust?"

Yes! The crowd replied in unison.

"That our very makeup has been arranged by the hands of a benevolent God? Or maybe a God not so benevolent?"

More ragged cheers rose.

"Have you ever thought, as you sit here today, that the person you *are* is not your *true* self, but instead a facsimile? That your very DNA holds inner secrets that have not yet been revealed?"

Yes!

"That you were meant to hold a far more impressive position in this world?"

Yes!

The gears at the bottom of the contraption gave loud grinding groans. Dexter Galaxy pushed his panicked palms harder against the clear walls, his handprints smearing the glass.

Good acting, Frisky thought. It was almost like Galaxy was afraid.

Altair the All-Knowing released his cape and raised both hands to the ceiling.

"Well, my friends! Watch and wonder as the Chaos Contraption reaches into the very atomic structure of good thespian Dexter Galaxy, rips him atom from atom, and reimagines him as his true self!"

Lights flared. Sound built to a crescendo.

It was time.

High above, Frisky let out an instinctive yowl and leaped into the air.

Paws spread. Claws extended. He struck a feline superhero flying pose, his tail whipping behind him as the air grew suddenly thick with ozone. The thrill of the descent clutched his throat. His fur rucked in the turbulent fall.

Through it all, Frisky kept his gaze on Dexter Galaxy's well-muscled shoulders.

His talons curled out to full extension, and the audience gasped at the sight of the gray cat falling from the rafters.

Crap! He was off target! Just a little, but also just enough.

Frisky gave one more yowl, then an ooooofff! as he thunked hard into the edge of the glass cylinder, bounced off the thick glass, then caromed away—luckily inside the tube—where he managed to finally sink a claw into the flesh of Galaxy's neck. The hold whipped him around, and angular momentum sent his solar plexus crashing into Galaxy's nose while his hind legs whipped around the actor's head.

The crowd went wild.

"Ahhh!" the magician's voice rose in the din, trying to regain control of the situation.

Rather than the projectors presenting a new image of Galaxy, as Altair had planned, the device Frisky hadn't been able to identify clicked and clacked.

The magician stumbled, and his concentration seemed to fade.

Screaming voices filled the hall with panicked trills. Something was wrong.

The Feral Sisters raced in from the wings, trying to pry the doors to the contraption open, but getting nowhere.

Inside the cylinder, Frisky grimaced and struggled

to catch his breath. He let go and fell to the contraption's floor, avoiding Galaxy's shuffling feet. "I meant to do that," he huffed in a tone as ragged as a gamma ray.

A blinding flash of orange and blue heat erupted from the pulse generators.

And for Frisky, everything went hyper-nova.

A moment later, the Chaos Contraption was empty.

Dexter Galaxy and Frisky the cat were both gone.

CHAPTER 5

On the cramped Warp 'n' Wail blues club stage, James bent the strings of his quasar-7 Meson guitar into the sound that Lyn had been laying down with the new multi-sonic hyper synthesizer he'd acquired thirdhand a week before. A moment later he stepped back and let his brother take the spotlight, which Lyn did, dancing to the four-bar beat, singing, and waving the scarred device like it was a ping-pong paddle.

The club felt out of time with the pristine aura that came from the rest of the spaceship.

Rather than touristy bright, the Warp 'n' Wail was dark and filled with shadow.

Instead of bright images of their next destination, peeling posterboards and yellowed photos adorned the walls. The tables were round and scarred, gleaming with stains from old liquor. The woodwork was stenciled with names like Moondog Malone, the Dutchman, Magic Max, and Muddy Waters, and while the microphones and sound system were modern in technology

—meaning adjustable and pitch-framed—they were embedded inside old-timey stainless-steel stands that were tall, spindly, and kind of fun to lean into. The stage was built with wooden floorboards that bent underfoot, too, which was another touch of realism that made James happy—it felt like the planks had been worn in by countless performers who had presumably graced its surface and they made wonderful tones of percussion when he stomped on them like a blues player did. The spotlight, too, flickered with nostalgic warmth, casting an amber glow over the weathered backdrop. The Warp 'n' Wail's air handling system piped in an engineered, almost sweet scent of old cigar and cigarette smoke that combined with the aroma of whiskey and gin to give the place a full sense of a real old-time blues joint.

He could almost hear the dusty voices of old players calling back and forth, sharing tall tales and throwing their heads back as they riffed the four-bar blues.

It was a fun place to play, even if James knew the façade was fake.

Still.

Where the hell was the cat?

Between furtive glances at the audience, James leaned into the rhythm and watched his brother pick up Victoria, his guitar, and take a new lead.

With Frisky growing later by the drink, the manager had drawn a line. Get up there or leave for good. So the brothers had gone on stage ten minutes ago to stall for time. It had worked, too. The club greeted them with wild and … fuzzy … applause. But ten minutes of a jam later, the locals were getting restless.

It was only a matter of time before they got pissed off enough to make them pay.

These cruisegoers were here to listen to Frisky do "I'm A Cat," among other things.

While Lyn had the advantage of being oblivious to anything outside himself, James understood that crowds of fans who weren't getting what they wanted were dangerous things to piss off.

He was getting worried.

James caught Lyn's gaze, and to his brother's credit, he could see the same question was on his face.

Where's the cat?

This was Frisky's show, after all. And it was *not* like Frisky to lose a chance to put the boys behind him. Had he overslept?

Between beats, a sharp crash came from double doors at the side of the room as they slammed open. The lights came on overly bright.

Voices reacted sharply.

A phalanx of official-looking officers flooded the room, causing no little grumbling and wailing.

Amid the chaos, James was so startled he almost fell off the platform.

Both brothers stopped playing, and both gaped out into the audience to see what was going on.

A screech of feedback came from the amplifier behind Lyn, making everyone wince until it calmed.

"Best thing you played all night!" a voice rose.

"Sorry to interrupt the show, folks," the leader of the security team said gruffly as they waded through the crowd and onto the stage. It was a tall Denebian, with more muscles than one would think could exist on a creature with so many folds of wrinkled purple skin. "But there's been a crime committed and we need to nab the offenders."

A hush settled.

The security officer turned to face the brothers.

"Lyn and James Moore, you're wanted for an inquiry regarding conspiracy in the suspected murder of both Dexter Galaxy and Frisky the Cat."

CHAPTER 6

Here we go again, James thought.

The security escort marched the boys through the twisty corridors leading to the captain's interrogation chamber. This was getting old. *Another cruise, another problem.* He leaned over and, tweaking a wistful corner of one lip upward in a half smile that he didn't feel, whispered to Lyn. "Are you all right? You haven't been this quiet since we swiped Mom's auto-jumper and crashed it into that satellite."

Back then they had been trying to jack into the comm stream of the Deep Phaser Array, a new band they'd just gotten into. Alas, the auto-jumper they swiped wasn't as auto as they'd planned and neither Lyn nor James could actually pilot the thing.

Mom had made them pay the damages.

Lyn turned his wide eyes to James. His lips moved, but he said nothing.

"Don't go *cat-a-tonic* on me now, brother," James quipped, hoping levity might help.

THE MAGICAL MYSTERY CRUISE!

Still nothing. Lyn had been struck senseless by the news of Frisky's demise.

Was it true? Had the cat been killed? If so, how had it happened?

Could it have been murder?

A shudder rolled down James's back.

Who would want Frisky dead?

The whole thing was too much for him, to be honest. His heart beat a billion parsecs a second and his skin prickled with anxiety.

Confusion and anger coursed through him. That horrible sense of dread that came from being uncertain of what was real made him anxious. Putting it all together with the obvious fact that the security detail had said both Frisky and Dexter Galaxy were dead… well… it all added up to say his brain was crashing into lockdown.

To be fair, nothing added up as far as James was concerned.

There were questions he didn't want to know the answers to — not the least of which was why this security detail had informed them of their rights to tell the captain the truth, the whole truth, and nothing but the truth, so help a pass through the airlocks.

The feeling was surreal.

Was it true? Were they suspects?

Then the door slid open, and James's stomach dropped like a rock in a black hole.

The dour expression on the face of Captain Leif Stewart, as he sat at the head of the oblong table, was enough to let James know his fears were in the right pocket. The boys had met the captain during their last cruise, and at one point, with Lyn unable to keep his mouth shut, Stewart had thrown them into the brig for safekeeping. Everything worked out well enough in the end, but James most certainly did not want to suffer a reprise version.

The captain was flanked by a pair of flunkies that included Calista Parallax, the ship's new Entertainment Director. She was a perfectly fit young Zendak who wore a professionally sharp pair of dark pants and a turquoise business tunic with a fashionably wide collar turned up at the corners. Gemlike implants glittered from each temple and connected her directly to the ship's extensive databases. Despite being all the rage with kids today, the implants gave James a gastric event. That Lyn stared at it with great intensity just made it worse. His brother had wanted to get one to help him tie his brain directly into the galaxy's entire music stockpile, something James was excited about too, though the idea of connecting directly to networks always gave him the creeps.

"There you are," Parallax said sharply as they stepped into the briefing room. "How good of you to show up somewhere on time."

"What do you mean?" James said.

"Don't pretend you weren't fifteen minutes late going on stage tonight."

"We were waiting for the cat!"

The director's face clouded.

Unlike the captain, the intense sense of confidence Parallax gave off was infused with a feeling of youthful vigor. She was a person of action. Her face was as smooth and clear as James remembered from their first brief meeting with her. The leanness of her body said she spent considerable time in the ship's fitness center. Given that James was unfamiliar with Zendak physiology, it was hard to assign her an age. But given the sharp aspect of her gaze, and the light shade of her purple skin, James was going with *older and more dangerous than she looked.*

Captain Stewart glanced up from his seat and grimaced. "Come. Sit down."

His ever-present shu-shu — a blotchy yellow, iguana-like creature with a long, slithery tongue that slipped into and out of its ridged lips as it tasted the stagnant air — sat in the crook of one arm.

Lillykins, James remembered. The shu-shu's name was Lillykins.

"Good little shu-shu," James said softly as he sat.

As the boys took chairs, the captain's fingers scratched Lillykins' chin, which was once again flaking and dry. Shadows darkened the captain's almost woody face and combined with the vivid lime-toned skin at his neck to make the commanding officer look like an avant-garde gargoyle — a terribly angry avant-garde gargoyle, but a gargoyle still. Deep creases in his command jacket said he'd been there too long. The curled edges of the captain's leafy, plantlike appendages said he could use better hydration.

"Can I get you a drink, sir?" James said as the security detail stepped away.

Stewart was from the Floradian system. He needed his water.

The captain gave him a smirk. "We will get to you next."

The interrogation center was too small to hold multiple suspects comfortably, but James realized then that Captain Stewart had already been applying his interrogation skills when the boys arrived. James did a double take when he recognized the two other suspects as none other than the shapeshifting sisters.

"Fae Feral?" Lyn said, snapping out of his funk as he took his seat. He spoke with more joviality than the situation called for.

"*Now* you decide to come out of it?" James said, suddenly worried about what his brother might say.

"I'm Doozie," the sister replied with an edge of condescension.

"Oh, sorry." Lyn blushed.

"Or you can call me Katrina, I guess," she said, casting an angry glance at the entertainment director. "That's my stage name for this tour."

"Hey, I'm Katrina," her sister snapped.

"Katrina?" Lyn said, still not getting the nuance of the moment.

"Sabrina and Katrina," James replied. "You know. Their stage names for the magic show."

"Oh. Yeah."

The girls glowered.

"That would make a great song," Lyn said. *"Sabrina Katrina, I'm so in love with you!"*

"Not now, Lyn," James snapped.

Despite himself a melody and a few lines for a new piece slipped into his mind, accompanied by a memory of the first moment he'd seen their act on stage. They were, he remembered, almost magical.

"This is not the *Green Nova* lounge social hour," the captain said. "Please constrain yourselves."

"If only it was," Fae moaned. "I'd kill for a Vumi high ball."

"Yeah," Lyn added. "And a Caboom tonic for me."

Fae gave a coy smile. "I figured you for a Caboom kinda guy."

"Ahem," the captain cleared his throat and the room calmed enough to hear air wheezing into the chamber softly, but far too slowly to make a difference.

Tension filled the space. Sweat formed on James's upper lip.

"So, back to our question," the man sitting to the captain's opposite side said, folding both hands at the edge of the table and indicating Fae. The blocky nature of his shoulders and the expanding thickness of his neck suddenly lent him an essence of intimidation. His eyes were dark as the vacuum, his hair buzzed short. The man's uniform was more blue than it was gray, and creased at the shoulders and collar, leading James to assume this was the ship's chief security officer. "What is your defense, young lady?"

"Our defense?"

"Yes. As we were noting before our interruption, Mr. All-Knowing filed a complaint in my office about your altercation with him at dress rehearsal. Now he's claiming you purposefully ruined the event in false retaliation."

"That just shows Altair is willing to throw *anybody* under the vacuum to save his reputation."

"You're saying Altair the All-Knowing is lying?"

"It was *his* contraption that disintegrated both a

galaxy-wide vidsie star and that odd little kitty. You tell me who's responsible."

"*Disintegrated?*" Lyn wailed.

"Where is that lech, anyway?" Fae said, ignoring Lyn. "He's the one you should be threatening to push out the airlock."

The chief security officer bunched his eyebrows. "Believe me, Miss Feral, we will investigate every angle of this event. Including the magician. But I find it unlikely to think he would do this to himself. If Altair is tainted with Dexter Galaxy's death, his career could be over."

"*His* career?" Fae wailed. "Just like a system man. What about *our* careers?"

"Yeah," Doozie added. "You're the one suggesting *we* killed Dexter Galaxy just so Fae could get even with Altair. What do you think *that* will do to *our* careers?"

"We're just getting started here, so I'm not saying anyone has done anything. But it would be a poor investigation that ruled out any possibility at this point."

"Investigation?" Lyn said, gazing at the officer through the tips of his bangs. "Are you the security officer?"

James shot a glance at his brother that urged him to shut up. Alas, he could already see his brother was unlikely to do something quite so intelligent.

The captain stopped petting Lillykins and raised a hand.

"I told you he was about as sharp as an asteroid," the entertainment director interjected, the interface embedded in her left temple glowed with a multicolored flare to indicate she was already accessing what was probably a massive internal Rolodex. "Can we just book the four of them and get it over with?" she said. "I've got replacement acts to find."

"What?" James said.

"Replacement acts?" Lyn added.

"I'm sorry, Calista, but Chief Officer Jabbert will manage this," the captain said.

Lyn opened his mouth, then shut it.

The officer leaned over to stare directly at Fae Feral. "So, what do you have to say?"

Fae remained adamant. "I say your accusation is offensive as hell. I can fight my own battles, thank you very much. And that means you can shove the idea that I would stoop to using Dexter Galaxy to get back at that low-life Altair the All-Leaching right up your cherry flavored—"

Doozie pressed a hand against her sister's forearm to shut her up.

"What my sister means to say is that we are just as interested in knowing what happened to Dexter Galaxy as anyone else is."

Officer Jabbert pursed his lips before continuing in a low tone. "Early word says we're pretty sure someone messed with the magician's device—something you had the opportunity to do. And," he paused for effect. "You are the ones who picked Galaxy from the audience. That makes you suspects A and B. If you didn't do it, I'd say you know who it is."

"We only picked him out of the crowd because he asked us to," Fae shot back.

"He asked you?" The captain cocked his head in

anticipation. "Are you suggesting Dexter Galaxy committed suicide?"

"I'm *suggesting* that we didn't know Dexter Galaxy was going to be in the audience until your security officer let us know he would be, and that he wanted to be picked as the volunteer."

"What security officer would that be?" Jabbert asked, his face showing disbelief.

"It's a poor investigator who doesn't even know the people who work in their office," Fae snapped back.

Doozie clasped her hand so hard onto Fae's arm that her sister winced.

"Don't worry about my sister," she said to both the captain and the entertainment director as well as Officer Jabbert. "She's had a day of it. But she's right about what happened. A security man came to us before the show. His uniform said he was a junior officer, so he's probably not on your radar screen. I think he was from Mr. Galaxy's detail. Said his name was Jones."

"There is no Officer Jones on my roster of agents."

Fae made her skin tone turn red and opened her mouth to reply, but Doozie was faster. "Are you sure?" she said. "His name was Lucifer. Officer Lucifer Jones."

"Lucifrous," Fae corrected.

"Oh, that's right." She pouted and turned her skin a velvety purple. "Lucifrous."

"I don't care if it's Lucifer, Lucifrous, or just Junior. I can say without doubt or reservation that there is no Officer Jones on the security roster."

"It happened, though," Doozie replied. "I swear it did. The observation deck is a publicly accessible location. There's got to be imagery, right? Check the ship's data logs and you'll see Officer Jones talked to us in the observation chamber pre-launch."

"You can bet I will," Jabbert said, clenching his fist.

"Then you'll see we're telling the truth." Fae sat back, crossing defiant arms over her belly, and expressing a metallic sheen that looked like a shield. "He was very hunky," she added.

"Hunky?"

"Tall, you know? Dark hair. Handsome. You won't be able to miss him."

"All right," Jabbert said as if to cut her off. A grin of satisfaction crawled over his face as he turned to take in the Moore brothers. His gaze lasered through to the back of James's skull. The pit of James's stomach fell, and his skin grew cold. "Let's say the conversation did occur. I'd say it's very curious, wouldn't you?"

"Curious?" James said before Lyn could jump in. "How so?"

"Without an official officer Jones on the register, I get to ask myself who benefits from all this, and if it's not the Feral Sisters, I'm coming up with only one answer. I'll give you three guesses and the first two don't count."

"I don't think *anyone* benefits!" Lyn wailed. "Especially not poor little Frisky!"

"I'm pretty sure you don't *think* about much of anything," entertainment director Parallax said.

"Hey!"

James pressed on. "That doesn't make sense, right? Why would we want our cat dead? Better yet an ultra-intelligent cat who was hooked into the entire galaxy's computer net? I mean, Frisky is a real pain in the butt, but those kinds of connections are helpful sometimes. And what's the deal with Dexter Galaxy, anyway? We don't know him at all. Why would we want him dead? The whole thing is insane."

"Good questions," Jabbert said.

"Come on, people," Parallax chimed in. "From where I sit, it's obvious. The cat who was in the process of stealing their place as a headliner got disintegrated by a high-profile magician, thereby saving the boys' place in the spotlight while destroying the careers of the cat, the actor, *and* the magician." Parallax turned her gaze to Doozie as if driving in a final failsafe on the airlock. "And it turns out that you and the assistants who picked out the target — and who *also* wanted to damage the magician — have a long history together. The only question then is whether you acted alone, hoping to frame the sisters, or whether you're acting together."

James locked eyes briefly with Doozie, and the two shared a moment of confusion.

"A long history together?" Doozie said.

"Come now, are you under the impression that I don't run background checks on all my entertainers or are you simply thinking that data of past interactions between the Feral Sisters and the Moore brothers is somehow hard to find?"

"I—"

"Because if so, I can tell you it is not. You shared a stage on the lunar moon, and then a room on your first cruise."

"We weren't sharing a room," Lyn blurted. "I was stowed away!"

"And that helps your case how?"

Lyn blanched, seeing the spot they might be in. "We were just roommates passing in the solar breeze." He looked at James with a suddenly bright expression. "Hey, that would make a great song too! *Solar breeze, burn up my mind ... fry my inner thoughts of summer ti-i-i-ime.*"

"Crap, Lyn," James said. "Concentrate."

Lyn gave a sheepish smile and hung his head before turning to the security officer. "Do you know what I had to do to keep them from ratting me out?"

Fae gave a wicked grin. "He's very bendy."

Lyn blushed. "Nothing compared to you!"

Then it was Fae's turn to blush.

James shook with anxiety. "Lyn," he said. His voice was calmer than he felt, but the sound of it now helped him shut down the feedback loops running wild in his head. He took a deep breath and calmed himself.

"Face the facts here," Parallax said. "The only reason you're on this cruise is because the cat saved Captain Stewart's bacon last time, and there wasn't time to get another talent director in time for this cruise."

"All right, director," Doozie added, raising her hands in surrender. "We fess up. We've run into the boys before, but nothing's going on here. We didn't even know they were on board this cruise until after agreeing to this gig and coming here."

"Neither did we!" James added. "And we don't know any Officer Jones, either."

Security Chief Jabbert gave a mournful sigh, then looked at the entertainment director, who shrugged, and then looked at the captain. "We could go around like this forever, sir. I'd say it's time to cut to the chase. It seems clear that the sisters are involved somehow, so I intend to keep them under wraps while my people finish our investigation."

"Under wraps?" Doozie said.

"You're locking us up?" Fae added.

"That's not fair," Lyn said.

"All right," Stewart said amid a cloud of shu-shu skin. "What about the brothers? Do we lock them up, too?"

The security investigator replied, "I don't have enough to keep them here. And that cat wasn't even supposed to be at the show, so I'm not sure how I can justify holding them." He turned to give James a bone-chilling stare. "But don't think that means you're off the hook. I'm assigning someone to check everything you've done since you got here. I promise that if you were involved, you're going down."

"What are you going to do about our act?" Fae said. "We've got a show to do."

"Never mind that, Captain," Calista Parallax added with a sense of youthful self-importance. "I've got a big Rolodex in the Space Cloud. We'll manage."

The doorway opened and four security systems slipped into the room.

"Fae and Doozie Feral," the captain said. "You are under ship arrest. The rest of you can leave now."

CHAPTER 7

For the briefest of instants, Frisky enjoyed the expressions on the audience's faces as Dexter Galaxy reacted to having been raked by his freefall. Shocked. Completely and fabulously shocked.

Hitting the floor of the Chaos Contraption, Frisky preened to them.

Then, just as his fur rose with the realization there was a third, unidentified figure in the device with him and Galaxy, a strobe flashed him with iridescent colors, a loud snap crackled through Frisky's ears, and a psychedelic wave of nausea bubbled up in his gut.

He yowled into the void. What direction was up? What was down?

Or all around?

Blazing lights flared.

A *whumpf* of fire burned in his brain as he seemed to fall through the cosmos.

Then the disoriented wail of the actor's screaming warbled over him in a gloppy, melted way that made it sound like it came from banks of liquified stereo studio speakers. Raw power frazzled his senses so completely that he was pretty sure he'd horked up the most dazzling hairball in all of existence just so he could watch it spin like a remote planet in the non-existence of the nothing that surrounded him.

The sense of nothingness clouded his brain worse than a lack of gravity ever could.

Like every cat of intelligence — meaning all cats — Frisky hated zero-g.

It was all there, though, every feeling amped up, every sensation burning.

He yowled into the void.

Then...

Blam!

His flank crashed hard into the ground, and there was nothing but the crushing pain of breath being kicked out of him.

I'm dead? Frisky thought. But then he snapped out of it: *I can't be dead. I'm a cat!*

Dead or not, he was certainly unable to breathe.

Panic burned in his nerves.

His solar plexus fought valiantly to rise, and when it did, a thin thread of air slipped into his lungs. *Air!* Sweet kitty goddess. *Fresh air! Yes!*

It was weird, though.

There was a distant aroma of freshly mown grass on a cool breeze that he did not like.

He opened his eyes and fought to take in another growly breath. A second, tiny squeak of air seeped into his lungs. A bigger breath later, Frisky blinked his eyes into focus well enough that he could make out the forms of people standing around him.

THE MAGICAL MYSTERY CRUISE!

"Free drinks to my free-dom!" A rich voice emanated from a small top-loading mini-fridge that flowed past. Its stainless-steel frame gleamed in the sunlight. The lid ratcheted open to reveal cold drinks stashed down in a bed of ice. *"Free drinks to my free-dom!"*

The face of a young woman filled Frisky's view.

She wore a plain striped skirt that fell to her knees and led to a pair of shiny leggings and worn shoes, clasped with magnetic strips that pulsed with a rainbow of color. Her top was a long-sleeved shirt decorated with red and orange patterns that shifted to magenta and teal as Frisky watched.

There were others here, too.

And…the sky! Looming so far up above!

Holy scratching post! Everything combined to make his fur ball up in batches.

As the crowd buzzed, Frisky hissed.

The databanks and holosimulators he'd connected to had said such things as open skies existed, but Frisky had never seen the real thing before. The idea that there was nothing overhead was frightening. Hyperventilation suddenly seemed like a great idea.

It was all still so freaky.

A stream of panic began to grow but, still feeling a little loopy from the crash, it was all Frisky could do to raise his head.

Leaning forward, the young woman peered at him.

She was a teenager. Long hair swinging in loose braids that were threaded through with a flashing line of white and purple lights. The lenses on her round-rimmed glasses snapped and flashed with a stream of data that piqued Frisky's curiosity. The frames slid down her nose, and she pushed them back up. "Wow," she breathed. "Far in."

There were at least ten others gathered around. Kids mostly.

"What the hell is that?" another one of them said, scratching the top of his head with one hand. The other hand held a placard that read *Blenders Are People, Too*.

A heavy chant came from somewhere nearby, adding depth to the crowd.

"Free the forks! Free the forks!"

There were a lot more than a dozen people here, Frisky realized. There was a whole crowd of people milling around on the grounds. He'd fallen into a gathering — a party of a sort, though no one seemed to be celebrating so much as chanting. Waves of voices echoed in Frisky's head, and the people here, all of them young and human, peered at him like he was on display.

Frisky didn't like it.

Shaking off the pain, he stood up, and with a whisk of his tail, got his balance back. At least nothing was broken, though now that his brain was clicking again he noticed a bent whisker drooping toward the grass.

"Damn it!" Frisky growled. "Do you know how long it took me to grow that?"

"It talked!" the girl screeched, pointing at him. Voices rose. "The cat talked!"

"Of course, I talked, you idiot!" Frisky said.

An odd hush rolled over the nearby crowd. A distance away, another presence stirred.

It was the other, extra figure from the Chaos Contraption — a big man dressed in one of *Marvel*'s

THE MAGICAL MYSTERY CRUISE!

uniforms — who was sprawled on the ground and extracting himself from where he'd been wrapped around the root system of a tree. Green leaves, curling toward orange, fell all around him.

Hoping to see who the officer was, Frisky touched his connection to the ship's data registers but the response was a cold, totally null return that made him worry *Marvel* might be gone.

Like some kind of dazed mummy, the man got up and brushed debris from his uniform jacket. He was tall and well-proportioned. Based on the stencils built into his uniform, he was part of *Marvel*'s security crew. The name "Jones" was stenciled on one of his shoulder patches.

At the same time, Dexter Galaxy also pushed himself up from where he'd crashed onto a table. The already rackety furniture was now crumpled below him, its spindly legs bent all cattywampus so that it looked to be a large, squashed beetle.

The actor rolled off the platform, groaning with pain.

Jaw agape, Galaxy straightened up. Blood rushed from his chiseled face leaving him pale. His expression formed into a sickening sense of wonder.

Frisky's gaze flitted from place to place, ears rotating to get a fuller sense of the area. His sniffer sniffed all the odors. From the ground, Frisky couldn't see much, but what he could take in was frightening.

He let out a huge cat sneeze.

They were in a neighborhood, standing on a grassy lawn whose aroma tickled his nose and made his eyes water. The street that ran past a distance away was built on a cul-de-sac, and almost certainly quiet in normal times, but now was filled with milling people and chanting voices. Tiered rows of well-weathered living pods lined the street, each pushed up against the other so closely they looked like the massive, sun-blasted tunnels built by some cities on planets without any atmosphere. They were painted what was once probably vibrant yellow, but that had now faded.

Whoever conceived this shindig had built a low stage at the open end of the street.

"I'm asking you to save the spatula!" an amplified voice came from a young man standing on the platform stage at the far end of the cul-de-sac. Cheers and chants rose.

"No flip, no flop!" the voices called in unison.

"I'm telling you to unchain the range!" the kid on the stage called back.

"Bake me, Poindexter Steckermann, you're our only hope!" the voices returned.

A mobile laundry machine on antigravity boosters zipped its autonomous way toward the stage, its warning buzzer blaring an obnoxious rhythm that matched the call-and-reply that was growing through the gathering. A top-loading dryer wobbled along beside it, its automated voice doing harmony with each of the crowd's rendition of *You're Our Only Hope*.

"Joe?" Dexter Galaxy said as a gawky young man came through the crowd to join the girl. He was tall and wiry, mostly elbows and knees. Dark hair coiled down to his shoulders, and a thin mat of a frizzy beard grew on his chin. A hawkish nose finished the image.

THE MAGICAL MYSTERY CRUISE!

"Who are you?" the young man said, taking Galaxy in as if he hadn't seen him there.

Galaxy's suddenly fevered eyes flitted from the mini-fridge to the crowd, and his jaw sagged into an expression that Frisky interpreted as horrible familiarity.

"No," Galaxy said. "It can't be."

"Where are we?" Frisky said.

"It's…"

When Galaxy didn't continue, Frisky growled. "What'sa matter — hound got your tongue? Out with it, man!"

"We're at 2907 Afton Glen Road," the actor finally said, calling loud enough to be heard over the din. "Audubon Sector."

"Like that helps," Frisky quipped.

"It's my home," Galaxy said, taking a deep breath and seeming to gain at least a little strength.

"You live in this dump? I thought you were famous or something."

"I did when I was a kid."

"That's freaky," Joe said.

"The machines are yours, right?" Dexter replied.

"Yeah. Poindexter helps out, but I make 'em in my garage."

Galaxy turned to the stage, and as he peered harder at the speaker, his face blanched even further.

Feeling claustrophobic about his view of feet and knees, Frisky took a run at Galaxy and launched himself. His claws sunk into the actor's hip and thigh, and using momentum and a properly leveraged hind leg, he scaled the actor's torso before coming to rest on his shoulder.

Galaxy yowled in pain, but Frisky managed to balance himself anyway.

"Much better," he said.

"Don't do that!" Galaxy called, nearly falling over.

The speaker stood on a ramshackle platform draped in sheets. He was young. Super-thin and gangly in the way of someone just out of their teenage years. His face glowed with an oily sheen, and even from the distance, Frisky could see that blotchy patches of acne covered the young man's face.

The speaker raised his fist. His voice was amplified by a wearable microphone.

"Listen to me now! Some of my best friends have been downloaded into appliances! Fred McManis is helping make a great toaster oven! And Melisade Mahnipande dedicated her intellect to the greatest lines of automated beverage dispensers in existence!" The crowd roared. *"You know it's true! We all have friends doing the same thing! And together, we're not going to let the Supreme Governor get away with this kind of atrocity!"*

"That's not an automated beverage dispenser, that's my wife!" Frisky quipped.

Kids around him chuckled.

"But seriously," Friskey continued, digging a claw in to balance on the actor's shoulder. "I'll tell you what an atrocity is. An atrocity is that this guy looks a lot like you! Minus the zits, anyway."

"It *is* me," Galaxy said. "Or at least it *was* me. I can't believe medical science hasn't cured pimples."

The girl who had been Frisky's first vision screeched and broke her longing gazes at the speaker to look at Dexter. "No way! You're not Poindexter Steckerman! Poindexter is way out. You're just an old guy. I should know, too. I'm his girlfriend."

"Poindexter?" Frisky said. "Your name is Poindexter?"

As the girl peered to get a second assessment of the actor, Galaxy took her in, then whispered so softly only Frisky could hear him. *Candi? Cripes, that's right! Candi McReary. I'd almost forgotten—"*

She shook her head with something that might have been appreciation. "What are you, like Poindexter's long-lost uncle or something?"

"Whaddaya mean 'it *was* you?'" Frisky said.

"I don't understand it," Galaxy said, pointing at the speaker. "But that's me. I'm, like twenty, right?"

"Poin-D is twenty-one," Candi said, her hand on her hip.

"This is unbelievable," Dexter said.

"You're saying we've gone back in time?" Frisky quipped.

"I … um …" Dexter Galaxy stammered for a moment, then pointed to where the speaker was extolling the value of intelligent air filter management and proper oxygen conditioning. "All I know for sure is that this is my very first rally. I'd recognize it anywhere. It's when I first began to see how much intelligent kitchenware activism needed to be done."

"Toasters are people, too," Candi said knowingly.

"This is very confusing," Galaxy said.

"I suppose it would be," Frisky said, almost sorry for the actor. His mind swirled in the moment, assessing all parameters and coming up with the only answer that made sense. It seemed certain that they had, indeed, when the Chaos Contraption did its glitch, or whatever that was, made some kind of temporal jump, gone back in time. Something more than twenty years. The kid out there — Poindexter Steckerman — was going to grow up to be the one and same Dexter Galaxy as the guy Frisky was currently digging his claws into.

Suddenly, Frisky's senses lurched.

He felt the motion rather than saw it — like he did when he was batting service bots down the vent ducts on *Marvel*, he saw a motion from a short distance away.

The officer. Jones. Fishing a device from his belt and then raising his arm in a sweeping motion that Frisky immediately interpreted as taking aim.

A plasma pistol!

The officer had a plasma pistol, and he was aiming straight for young Mister Steckerman!

"Die, you scoundrel!" Officer Jones cried.

But as the officer locked his weapon down, and as his thumb twitched over the triggering button, Frisky leaped into the air, flying over the heads of several of the onlookers, who were oblivious to the full situation.

But Frisky understood.

He soared, forepaws extended and wide, claws in a "full rake" position.

He landed on the officer's forearm, and as the shot went wide right, Frisky sank both claws and teeth into the material of the officer's jacket.

A wild scuffle erupted.

Voices called.

Accusations and grunts and screams came.

Somewhere in there, Officer Jones got his hand wrapped around Frisky's throat. Only a well-placed back claw to the cheekbone saved him from having his head popped off. In the distance, though, Frisky felt his mind reach out to a device he could sense immediately as a toaster oven.

A connection snapped the synapses in his mind to attention. A billion cycles flowed in an instant and a protocol connection filled his mind.

A voice came, then, thin and reedy.

Watch out!

Frisky snapped to consciousness just in time to see Jones's fist, clutching the butt of his plasma gun, falling toward him.

He scampered away, barely missing the blow and landing on all four feet, claws splayed and ears pinned back.

Frisky pulled on his link to the toaster oven, feeling other appliances joining the network now.

"Get him," Frisky called.

A moment later the toaster oven, its elements glowing orange hot, fell onto Officer Jones.

The man screamed, and as the washer and dryer they'd seen earlier entered the fray, the officer, in no little pain, ran off.

"What the hell was that?" Dexter Galaxy said as things settled.

Frisky was seated now. He licked a paw to groom

himself, acting in every way as if what had just happened was the most natural thing in the world.

"That," Frisky replied, "Is why kitchenware activism is such a good idea."

"You're welcome, Leader," the appliance said through Frisky's link. *"How may we serve you?"*

CHAPTER 8

Despite himself, even as they were stepping out of the captain's operations center and into the interconnected network of service hallways that connected the ship, the song came to James. Or at least a big part of it. The whole opening and chorus arrived so firmly that even the clattering echo of their bootsteps against the barren walls couldn't shake it. He didn't know how busy he wanted the bass line to be, and there was the question of how hard to wail on the outro, but he felt it all. A to G, then G-flat. The chorus in E. The bridge was a C that slid up to D. Maybe they'd have to lay down a couple of different threads to tie it together, but that would be fun.

He felt it all so strongly that he broke out in a light hum, then sang a touch.

"*Sabrina Katrina,*
You make me feel like a millionaire, Ya!
Sabrina Katrina,
Make me feel like I'm floating on air, Ya!"

"I love it!" Lyn said, his big eyes staring out from

under the mop of blond hair that fell over them. "Ya got any more?"

"I think it's all there. I just wish I had a guitar to set it down."

That was how it worked for him. Play something and it became real. Walking down the utilitarian and cramped service hallway and toward the main passenger hub, he sighed.

"You okay, brother?" Lyn said.

"Yeah. I'm fine."

"You don't look fine."

They came to the main doors. It was now officially late in the standard ship "day" but James knew the place would be cram-packed with throngs of fans of every magician in the galaxy. Before they got here, the idea of a magical cruise sounded like fun. Now …

"I'm just feeling a little claustrophobic, you know?"

Lyn pushed the door lever, and it irised open to reveal the throngs of people in the central chamber where all the spokes that led to all the decks came together into one grand atrium. At the center of the floorplan was the *Green Nebula*, that social center that Captain Stewart had noted in their interrogation. It was a dynamically configured bar that morphed its shape based on the time of day and the sounds around it. Right now half of it was some kind of rainforest, the other half a razz club, complete with purple and blue strobes. The smell of the rainforest was fresh and clean, though, something that hit James in the right place about now. Mostly he was glad that there wasn't a zero-g thing going on right now. He had a song to get down.

He was not in the mood to share zero-g with a couple thousand of his closest friends.

"I get it," Lyn said as he led them into the masses of wizard followers, many of whom were dressed for the part. "It's a lot of people."

James scoffed, then followed his brother. He was happy they were dressed for the blues club rather than wearing their flashy Intergalactic Band of Brilliance regalia. He didn't want to stand out. "Yeah," James called out to Lyn as he raced ahead of him. "Good luck for the security guys finding 'Lucifrous Jones' in this mess, right?" he called again.

Oof.

Lyn came to such an abrupt halt that James crashed into him.

"That's the answer!" Lyn called as the two clung to one another to keep from falling.

All eyes in the area around them swiveled to them.

Lyn, of course, took a deep bow.

"What's the answer?" James said when things had returned to normal.

"Officer Jones holds the secret to what's going on in this case. All we have to do is to find him and we find the culprit!"

James frowned, in disbelief. "I think you're actually right."

"You don't have to sound so surprised."

But James's mind was running now.

"We know Frisky didn't mean to miss the gig," Lyn said.

"Of course not. The cat would do anything to rub our noses in his show. No one could have known Frisky would be there, so he couldn't be the target. And this Lucifer guy is the one who keyed the sisters onto Galaxy."

"Lucifrous," Lyn corrected James.

James ignored his brother. Blood was pumping now. There would be time to give him hell for it later. "If we track down that security agent — if that's even what he was — then the truth of what's going on will probably come out."

Lyn set his face into a grievous expression. "I want to see whoever killed my cat burn in the darkest gaps of a black hole!"

James nodded. He wasn't sure he'd go that far, but his brother had a point. Frisky may well be a pain in the ass, but he was their pain in the ass, and he didn't like the idea of anyone killing Frisky, regardless of how much of a jerk the cat could be at times.

That said, he hadn't gotten the feeling that Officer Jabbert had put much credence in the existence of one Lucifrous Jones. The feeling of the song he'd just been gifted reverberated inside him, and he heard the chorus again.

Sabrina Katina, I'm so in love with you!

Maybe that would work, and maybe it wouldn't, but James was struck by a sense of injustice in it all. The image of the sisters locked in some kind of stasis gave him a headache. "I'm pretty sure Jabbert thinks the girls are just making Jones up."

"But they aren't!"

"I don't think so either. But if I'm right that means it's up to us to find Jones."

"I agree."

"Otherwise, I think the coppers are going to railroad the girls into a lifetime in jail."

Lyn's face clouded. "We can't let that happen."

As the song poured itself over James's mind, he knew that guitar or not, he would never forget it.

"You're right again," he said. "We've got to figure this one out on our own."

"Free the sisters!" Lyn said, thrusting a fist into the air. When it drew the attention of a couple hundred magician nuts, he did it again. "Free the sisters!"

This time James didn't even mind.

CHAPTER 9

Frisky sneezed.

Sitting sphinxlike on the abysmal grassy lawn but basking in the warmth of the sunlight under that most intimidating of blue skies, Frisky managed to feel properly indulgent and in his place, overseeing the world as the fleet of intelligent machines, Joe, Poindexter, and Dexter Galaxy did all the work to clean up after the event.

"I can't believe these appliances did that," Joe said. "I didn't build them for self-defense, but I like it."

"Life finds a way," Dexter replied. "Believe me."

Frisky sneezed again, then rubbed a paw over his runny nose, feeling more miserable as the moments passed. Kitty snot matted its way into the hair of his forepaw.

"Are you okay?" Dexter said after his last sneeze.

"I'm fine," Frisky said. "I meant to do that."

Galaxy laughed, which annoyed Frisky to no end.

Being allergic to grass wasn't bad enough. His sinuses closed further with each passing moment.

THE MAGICAL MYSTERY CRUISE!

The commotion died down shortly after the security officer had fled. Poindexter finished off his speech quickly, but with a rousing "They can't keep me down!"

Despite that stirring conclusion, the crowd dispensed more rapidly than others might have, which was fine by Frisky. He had things to think through, and while his brain was still working faster than the normal sentient being, he found it frustrating to be separated from the ship's computer systems. He missed the network.

"It's amazing what a death threat will do to clear the streets," Frisky said, surveying the empty cul-de-sac.

Even Candi, the love of Poindexter's life, had slipped away.

"I'd take that as a sign it's not going to work out," Dexter said to Poindexter.

"But we're in love," the younger Dex argued. "We're going to be together forever."

"Trust me, kid," the older Galaxy said as he folded chairs and pulled tarps off tables. "I know she's a great kisser, but if the fact that she isn't here now isn't proof enough that it's time to move on, then I don't know what is."

Poindexter's pimply face flushed cherry red. "Who are you?"

"I'm you."

The teenager took one look at the futuristic actor's chiseled body and augmented vidsie looks and scoffed. "No, my man, you are most definitely not me."

"Give it time."

"Yeah. Sure. Next thing you know you'll be telling

me I get all the girls." He looked whimsically down the path where Candi McReary had left.

"Yeah, you will," Dexter replied. "And some of the guys, too."

That took Poindexter back a bit, but after a moment he shrugged and moved on. "I don't understand."

"Crap, kid. Get with the program," Frisky quipped, then sneezed again. "We're from the future. And we're here to save your ass."

"You're from the future?"

"You're a very good listener," Frisky said. It was a stupid question, but at least Poindexter Steckerman had moved on from trying to comprehend how Frisky could talk. For all their hubris, humans were not particularly bright.

"How old are you?" Poindexter asked the actor.

"Forty-five standards," Dexter replied. "That means if my math is right—which we both know has never been my strong suit—I'm twenty-four years ahead of you."

"Twenty-four years?"

"If my math is right."

The teenager contemplated for a moment, then fell limply onto a folding chair.

Frisky sneezed again. "Goddamn it!"

"I can't believe it," Poindexter said. Then he looked up with expectation. "Did I save the appliances?"

"Kind of," Dexter replied. A sudden expression of glee came over his face, though. "The battle's not over by a long shot, but things are coming along, you know? Being here and seeing where it all started is making me feel good about how much progress we've made.

There's still a lot of work left to change hearts and minds, but at least machine sentients have legal rights in almost every civilized system."

The Roomba gave a warm but startled beep, and Frisky felt a new energy build in its circuits.

Poindexter leaned over and toggled the automatic disintegration tabs of several empty drink dispensers. The grimace on his face as they composted themselves in real-time let Frisky know the kid was wondering why the people who drank the drinks didn't just do that themselves. It only took a moment. A sigh said he understood more about human nature than the usual teenager did, something that made Frisky think twice about the elder vidsie star. Maybe there was more to him than his external perception suggested. Thinking harder, Frisky reached out through his new link to direct the vacuum cleaner over to finish picking up debris on the street—a task it immediately whirred away at.

"I still don't get it," Poindexter said, standing up and pacing now. "I mean. Okay. You're from the future. But why are you here now?"

Galaxy began to answer. "Um. Well." It was clear he had no answer, which made sense. All he knew was that he stepped into All-Knowing's Chaos Contraption and next thing he knew, bam! Here he was.

But Frisky's brain ran cycles over cycles.

He replayed the moment of his leap and played back over saved sensors as he twisted, falling through the air and focusing on the actor's back and shoulder as Altair the All-Knowing ran through his stupid patter. As he fell, he saw the shadow that was the officer come near the Chaos Contraption. That he took care to avoid the visible portions of the floor told Frisky this unknown officer knew what he was doing.

And as the bits and bytes built in his head, the information came together to form an idea.

"It's the Hitler thing," Frisky blurted, the full supposition forming even as he spoke.

Both the young and old Poindexters stared at him stupidly.

"Hitler?" Poindexter said.

"Despot," Frisky snapped. "Horrible human being. Long time back. Started a big war, then killed himself."

"What about his thing?" Dexter said.

"The less said about his thing the better, I'd guess," Poindexter said, suddenly giggling a teenaged chortle.

Frisky hissed. "Enough frivolity."

The pair silenced.

"After he caused a horrible war, a bunch of people made up stories about how, if they could go back in time, they would kill Hitler and stop the war from ever happening."

"Ah." Poindexter scratched his head. "I don't get it."

Frisky pointed a paw at Poindexter and extended a claw. "They want you dead."

"What?" Dexter replied.

"The guy took a shot at you, right? Plasma weapons aren't anything to scoff at. Whoever is doing this wants your younger self dead."

"Why?"

"I'd guess someone thinks you've been too successful."

"I don't understand—" Poindexter started.

But Dexter interrupted with a fervor that said he was catching on.

"The opposition is intense, little me. I mean. We've got some real enemies now, with pockets deep as black holes. I know it doesn't feel like that right now, because right now you're nothing. Just a kid doing what you think is right. You see this as some kind of theoretical game but believe me when I say that you'll come to see the reality of it all as time goes by. These people are serious when they say appliance super-intelligence shouldn't have rights. You'll lose a lot of friends by making that argument. But I think all this happening means that we've made too many inroads. We're winning and they don't like it."

"Right," Frisky said. He blinked back tears and realized that he wanted to rub his eyes more than he'd ever wanted anything in the world.

"This attack is interesting, though." Dexter sat back with an odd sense of satisfaction.

"How so?" Frisky said.

"It's the first time anyone wanted me dead for being too successful."

Poindexter gulped. "You say that as if there have been other times people wanted you … me … dead."

"Usually, it's because I stole someone's girlfriend or significant other."

"Seriously?" Poindexter seemed suddenly intrigued.

"It's not as glamorous as you might think."

But Poindexter's expression said he thought it most surely would be exactly as glamorous as it sounded. Then a cloud came over his face. "But if they kill me, won't that kill you, too?"

The question brought Dexter up short.

"That's the whole idea on the Hitler thing, really," Frisky said. He cleared his throat, and for a minute thought he could breathe again "The grandfather paradox."

"Hitler was a grandfather?" Poindexter said. The conversation was stretching his ability to cope.

"Never mind," Frisky said, twisting a whisker and feeling a sneeze come on. "I swear you people can't keep with what's important. It's like you're all ADHDed all the time."

"That's fat coming from a cat."

Frisky changed the topic.

"All this is great, but the most important thing now is that if we're going to figure out what's happening, we need to chase down the officer, then threaten to rip out his throat if he doesn't tell us who sent him and how."

"Rip out his throat?" Dexter's cheeks had paled.

Frisky blinked. "Did I say that?"

"You did."

"Sorry. I try to keep cat idioms to myself."

"Is that how you actually think?"

"Only when it's deserved. But that's not the point again. The point is that we need to figure this out or we're never getting back to our timeline. That has to be what's going on, right? Unless this was some kind of timeline suicide mission, the guy who came through with us was going to kill Poindexter, thereby kill you, too, then hightail it back to the future. That means he's gotta have a way back home or he wouldn't have come here in the first place."

THE MAGICAL MYSTERY CRUISE!

"That makes sense." Dexter pressed his lips together.

In the distance, the appliances finished cleaning up the grounds, and another robot finished folding up the sheets and tablecloths. When the robot finished, it rolled to Dexter's side and leaned into him. The device came to Dexter's waist.

"I think you have an admirer," Frisky said.

The robot flashed a thin magenta light that circled its skullcap of a top shelf.

Dexter seemed frozen for an instant, then let his hand fall to scratch it.

The robot shuddered and Frisky felt a sense of contentment swell over the little network he'd created.

"So," Dexter said. "How are we going to find the guy who attacked Poindexter?"

Poindexter broke in, standing tall and thin in his sneakers. "We use me as bait."

"I don't like the sound of that," Dexter said.

"It makes sense, though," Frisky said. "If you want to catch a mouse, you gotta put down a little cheese."

"That's stupid," Dexter said.

"Only if you're the mouse."

Dexter chuffed derisively.

"You got a better idea?" Poindexter said.

Dexter put his head in his hands, then looked at Poindexter. "I don't want you dying here, you know? I've got skin in this game."

Frisky was beginning to like this Galaxy guy or at least the younger version of him.

"Yeah," Poindexter said. "But unfortunately for me, it's not your skin that has to be the bait."

"Last I looked, your skin is my skin," Dexter said.

"I guess that's fair enough." Poindexter looked at the actor, then ran his fingertips over his oily skin as if in wonder. "I admit that's still hard to believe."

Dexter shrugged. "All right," he said. "The idea is presented and approved. Poindexter is the bait. Now we just have to figure out where to put the hook."

Frisky glanced at the driveway that led from an open garage. The intelligent washer, dryer, mini-fridge, and vacuum cleaner were all standing at attention, guidance panels flashing with a series of signals that Frisky heard as commentary.

"What should we do next, master?" the washer said through the feed.

He stood on all fours and shook out his fur. A huge sneeze later, he focused on the appliances.

They were from the past, so their interfaces and protocols felt simple to the point of being childlike. But they were here, and they were active. The power of their desire to be of service was as strong as anything Frisky had encountered before.

"I've got an idea," Frisky said.

Then he turned to the appliances.

"Do you all have any friends?"

CHAPTER 10

Yes, James thought as he sat upright in the pool's lounge chair. The sounds that had been filling his thoughts died down. He had the solo down now, and though the bass groove was still being elusive, everything else was there musically. He liked the *"I would come undone,"* thing his brain had added, too. He loved it when that happened.

He breathed deeply, happy for once.

The song had been picking at him incessantly, and he knew it was going to be good.

Sabrina Katrina. Yeah. He liked it.

He still needed a stanza, of course. One more set of lyrics and he'd present it to Lyn to see what he thought. But Lyn would like it, or else. The girls were playing on his mind as the day wore on. It made him mad to think of them stuck in *Marvel*'s brig, obviously falsely charged, when they should be out and doing their more than amazing art.

It didn't help that nothing they had tried was shedding any light on the case.

"I don't know where else to go," Lyn said from his chaise lounge.

They were back at the pool, sitting alone against the farthest wall where visibility out was good, but the ability to pry inward was not so much. The sound of voices echoing over water droned on. Lyn peered over the pool, shielding his gaze from the artificial sun because he'd forgotten to bring his sunshades.

"You're sure you didn't get anything from the cafeteria workers?" James asked again.

While James had spent the middle of the day trying to scrounge information from various security officers stationed around the ship, Lyn had been responsible for sidling up to the service staff. Both were hoping to shake loose information on a tall, somewhat hunky security officer with black hair who might or might not have been assigned to Altair the All-Knowing's show. Earlier they'd both teamed up to chat with the stage crew during their sound check for tonight's show, but it was obvious no one knew anything—or at least obvious no one was talking if they did. Turned out that neither the service staff nor the random security goon had much else to add.

As far as James could tell, there was no Lucifrous Jones on the cruise.

"Not a thing," Lyn moaned in response, sipping a chilled combination of orange juice and Palauan boysenberry ice cream. It came lined with crushed shavings of something the lounge called maple syrup cubes but were really just sugar-infused sugar. The swizzle stick was a rod of pure chocolate that had skewered a high-density cherry that had been coated with powdered sugar.

"I don't think you need that much energy, brother," James said when Lyn had first ordered it.

"Well," Lyn had quipped as he finalized the order. "I think you're insane and look where that's got us."

Sometimes being with Lyn was like being with a twelve-year-old.

Now, after having consumed half of the drink, Lyn was a mess of emotions, and his hands were shaking with the need to release pent-up energy. "There's g-g-g-got to be a way to s-s-s-save the girls and find my k-k-k-kitty," he cried, stammering with massive sugar overload. He lay back on the chaise lounge and put his hand dramatically over his forehead.

James sighed and peered over the pool section.

"Oh crap."

Lyn perked up and followed James's gaze to see Calista Parallax, the cruise's new entertainment director, picking her determined way through the patchwork of tables and chairs, obviously headed their way. "What's she doing here?"

"I don't know," James replied, "but I have a feeling we're about to find out."

The boys both sat up straighter.

"Good afternoon," Parallax said as she came to a stop at the foot of their lounges.

"Director Parallax, how good to see you," James replied.

Parallax took a moment to scan the area around them. "Trying to hide away, I see."

"Just catching a few calm moments before the show

tonight," James replied. "We find it good to calm the nerves before big shows."

"R-r-right-o," Lyn said, raising his glass. "A little calmness n-n-never hurt anyone, right?"

Parallax, perplexed, stared at Lyn.

James cleared his throat to divert her attention. "What can we do for you?"

"With both the Feral Sisters and your cat currently unable to perform, I'm going to need you to cover their bases."

"I thought you had a big R-r-rolodex in the Sp-p-pace Cloud," Lyn snapped back.

"No time," Parallax said. She locked eyes with James. "Is he all right?"

James shrugged.

The edge of her voice could cut Malgarian crystal, which he took as a warning. Lyn, however, wasn't as adroit. He crunched up the last of his swizzle stick.

"B-b-but I heard you say it. 'Don't worry, Captain. I've got a big Rolodex in the Space Cloud.' What happened?"

Parallax clenched her fist but said nothing for a long beat.

"You need us to play three shows?" James said. "I'm not sure we can do that. I mean, the Sisters and Frisky's acts are cross scheduled." He didn't need to tell Parallax that he'd complained about that to begin with—that her approach to programming made fans choose one or the other, and that this was bad business.

"I like competition," Parallax replied then. *"I want my acts to be on their best face, and competition for viewers drives you to your best."*

THE MAGICAL MYSTERY CRUISE!

It was bullshit, of course. Artists did art. And artists were already a mass of insecurity all by themselves. Adding her kind of pressure didn't usually help one way or the other.

"So, you'll have to split up," she said. "One of you take the cat's gig, the other the girls."

"W-w-w-wouldn't it be easier to just let t-t-them out?" Lyn spat in sugary spasms.

By the sound of his brother's stutter, James was beginning to wonder if the drink had been cut with something harder.

"No," Director Parallax said. She put a hand on her hip and glared at Lyn. "It's a lot easier simply to have you do all the shows or ensure you that you'll never work again."

"Hah!" Lyn said even as James started to reply.

"Don't toy with me." Parallax's gaze turned venomous.

"I know," Lyn said, capitulating with a pair of raised hands. "D-d-don't play with you or you'll point that b-big Rolodex on us."

"I'm warning you. Do not mistake a lack of time with a lack of ability," the entertainment director said. "I can make your life hell."

She wasn't joking. The name Calista Parallax had been floating around the industry for a few standard years. She was a mover and a shaker. Being young in the business meant she could be impetuous, but her reputation was on the rise. It would be good for business to stay on her bright side.

"I'm sure my brother is just under the influence of

sugar, director. He doesn't mean anything. We are here to help."

"That's what I like to hear."

"Do you care who takes which gig?"

She stared at the twins, then laughed. "As if anyone can tell which is which."

James shrugged. "Sounds good."

"C-c-call us what you want as long as the ch-ch-checks clear," Lyn added. His expression had darkened for a moment when he realized James was capitulating. Now he was back on his game again. "At least we'll make some extra grub."

"You'll have to work that out with Frisky and the girls," Parallax said.

"You're n-n-n-not c-c-c-cutting us another check?"

"It's your friends and your cat who got us into this. Work it out with them."

James put his hand up to forestall another response from his sugared-out brother.

"We'll make it happen," he said.

"Good."

Then Parallax strode away and the Moore brothers were alone again.

"Sh-sh-she can't do th-th-that to us!" Lyn said, finally letting loose the steam that had been building.

"Apparently she can," James said.

"I'm not p-putting up with it." He ran his hand through his hair. "My god, my hair is tingling. Is your hair tingling, brother?"

James grunted. "You don't have a choice."

Lyn dashed down the last of his drink, then stood up so rapidly he nearly pitched forward. His unbuttoned shirttails wrapped around him. "You always h-ave a choice, b-brother. You always have a ch-ch-ch … option."

With that, Lyn was gone, racing through the crowd of people at the pool like he had a pair of rockets on his feet.

James leaped up and tried to follow him.

He had to run to do it.

Luckily he made it to the exit locks in just enough time to see Lyn's flowing shirttails disappear down the main corridor to the right.

James picked his way through the crowd like a skier on a downhill course.

"Lyn!" he called. Desperation filled him now. "Lyn!"

His brother stepped into a lift tube at the end of the hall. James put on a burst of speed and barely made it into the pod before the door irised shut. Panting, he caught his breath and ignored the stares of their fellow travelers. They were a pair of older visitors and three of Altair the All-Knowing's sycophants, each wearing a top with a glittering holographic pad that spewed archaically dense self-help edicts. "You are what you dream," scrolled one. "Eat at your own pace," said another. "Be the World," said the third.

"Going down," a voice said.

The pod moved.

"Down?" said one of the sycophants. "I thought we were going up?"

James bent to his brother and grabbed up his shirt collar in one hand. "What are you doing?" he said through clenched teeth.

"I'm reporting Calista P-P-Parallax to the Chief Security Officer."

"Reporting her?" James thought his head might explode.

"Illegal b-b-b-business p-p-p-practices," Lyn said. "And bullying."

"Are you out of your mind?"

"It's an o-open and sh-shut case."

The lift tube door opened.

"Th-th-this is our floor."

James let go of Lyn's collar, and as the pair got off the tube, Lyn adjusted his shirt accordingly. Then Lyn turned to the sycophants and, before the door closed behind them, said, "F-f-f-fear not, fellow travelers, up is d-d-down and d-down is up."

Two of them gave a similar hand gesture that James understood was some kind of signal.

Lyn replied in similar terms.

The door closed and the lift tube went on its way.

"What was that?" James said, giving the signal.

"How am I supposed to kn-kn-know?" Lyn replied. "Those people are crazy."

Then Lyn was off again, slipping down the hallway toward the security command offices.

James dashed off behind him, unable to close the distance until Lyn ducked into an open doorway.

A moment later, James found himself in the open reception area of the Security Command Office.

Beyond the attendants' desk was an open pit, sectioned off by a wavering forcefield set to have just enough movement to ensure people knew it was there —protecting the officers from any untoward attack—

but easily able to be seen through. Cruise Security was always trying to make the guests feel comfortable, and such transparency was part of the package.

Three officers were behind the field, each employed doing something at their desks.

A fleet of robotic mechs floated from station to station.

The walls displayed views from a randomly shifting set of 3D cameras staged around the ship. In the middle of the pit was a deep holographic image of *Marvel*'s flight path. Their next destination showed as less than a standard day's travel away.

"What can I do for you," said a perfectly put-together holographic administrator.

The artificial element had been designed to present itself as whatever species had approached it, so the administrator was now a cleanly coifed human of an age perhaps a year younger than Lyn. Pretty. If she hadn't looked altogether competent, James would have thought her to be just Lyn's type.

Score one for the AI.

"I want to t-talk to the chief," Lyn replied.

"I'm sorry, but the chief is occupied."

"He'll want to see me. I need to report a c-crime!"

James was happy to see that his brother's sugar high seemed to have been mostly run off.

"In that case, please fill out a form Zed-63-12 and submit it to the investigations committee." A holographic form appeared before Lyn.

Realizing his brother was going to get a classic bureaucratic run-around, and that at least he was occupied now, James slipped away from the conversation.

The chief's office was a short distance back from the attendant's desk. The door was closed, but in that same vein of transparency, the door was made mostly of clear composite so that he could peer in.

Which James proceeded to do.

There.

He saw it.

On the chief's desk.

It was a device of some sort, a small dark box with a pair of wires coming from it. A light at its top cycled slowly through red, blue, and green tones. James felt drawn to it. Like it was somehow important. In the process, he recalled the conversation in the captain's briefing room. Something had gone wrong in the Chaos Contraption right as Dexter Galaxy and Frisky had been fried. A device in Altair the All-Knowing's Chaos Contraption had been fiddled with.

Could this be that device?

The chief was in his office, too. He sat on one side of the desk that held the device and was having a conversation with a technician of some sort who was sitting across from him. The chief's neck, bulging in normal time, seemed extended and red. His eyes carried a sharpness that James was happy to not be on the other side of.

The tech, on the other hand, shrank down into his chair.

The chief said something even more firmly than before.

James sat back, stunned. He was no lip reader, but it was hard to miss this one.

THE MAGICAL MYSTERY CRUISE!

Get. Rid. Of. It, the chief had said, clearly indicating the device.

The idea sat on his mind like a pile of clay. Wasn't that device evidence?

Yes. James was sure it was.

And wasn't getting rid of evidence a major problem — especially for a security officer in charge of an investigation?

Yes.

Thou shalt not mess with evidence.

He was sure he'd read that somewhere, and quite certain it had to be written down in some dusty manual somewhere.

The device had done something. Tripped a wire or toggled a switch. James drew a silent breath, knowing it was important, and surprised to find he wanted to get his hands on it.

A phrase came to him.

As you raise the curtain, crowd unaware,

Dressed in sparkle wear, you pass the key and trip the trap door.

That was it! The last stanza to "Sabrina Katrina." Or at least part of the last stanza.

In the remote cloud of space, James heard his brother, still arguing with the attendant, and as Lyn's voice went on and on, he watched as the tech, shaken now, got slowly to his feet, gently picked up the small device, and shoved it into his pocket.

The office door slid back as the tech approached.

"Have a nice evening, Harv," the Chief said, his voice still edged.

"I will," the tech promised. Then he paused and

patted the pocket where he'd just stashed the device. "Don't worry about a thing."

Not wanting to be seen, James stepped away quickly.

"Come on," he said to Lyn, taking him by the armpit and shoving him toward the Command's door.

"But I'm not done here!"

"Yes, brother, you are."

James yanked hard to pull Lyn's fingers from the doorframe. He had a technician to trail. There was no time to waste.

CHAPTER 11

Less than an hour after the rally and following a chittering of directions that came across the local network Frisky had created among all the intelligent appliances in the nearby neighborhood, Frisky directed both Poindexters through the quiet streets of Dexter's old neighborhood and into a business district shopping zone where a nearby Eat, Play, Wash Grill and Fun Room was doing brisk business. It was one of the multipurpose buildings that had sprung up in the period, which was a popular approach since it cut the costs of real estate by the number of shops in any single building. The grouping of Eat, Play, Wash was a better conglomerate than one might think—a place where parents could take their kids to play while both eating and getting their laundry done.

It was crowded now.

Maybe thirty families of various sizes, eating pizza or hoagies and playing games while getting their weekly chores done.

Not that Frisky cared about any of that.

He was hungry. And the food generator here on past Earth made a good pass at chicken meats. Mostly, though, all Frisky cared about was that the place had glass walls, so it would be easy for the would-be assassin who had followed them to this time period to spot them. The fact that it was indoors and Frisky didn't have to breathe in the annoying odor of raw grass was a great side benefit.

Just a minute after arriving, Frisky already felt better.

He had jacked into a network of smart appliances, which showed him that said assassin had retreated to a place nearby. A security camera gave Frisky its feed, and a few minutes later the three were entering Eat, Play, Wash.

Since the goal was to get the killer to come get them, both Frisky and Dexter made enough of a clatter to attract the assassin's attention, and in they went.

The Eat, Play, Wash was a big, open place that smelled of an oddly comforting combination of bread, condiments, plastic, cold cuts, and warm linen. They ordered their food — salami wrap and cinnamon-fried potato mash for Poindexter, a salad for Dexter, complete with an oil and vinegar dressing since the place didn't stock Arcturan balsamic. Straight chicken meats for Frisky. Then the humans took seats and Frisky sat on the table to eat, all of them out in the open, waiting.

It didn't take long.

The assassin had been sitting in a park, studying maps, and probably making Plan B on his mission when first an emergency beacon tested itself, drawing his attention to the building. When that didn't work, a series of automated transit systems glommed together and created a ruckus. That was finally enough to focus the assassin's attention long enough that he saw into the building.

The traffic control sensor contacted Frisky first.
Subject Incoming.
Frisky tweaked a whisker.

"He's here," Frisky said, just as the entry tone buzzed.

The assassin walked in, tall and dark with a sharp chin and hard eyes. His uniform jacket was unbuttoned now and hanging loose, though the weight of his plasma blaster weighed down the side where he slipped his hand into the pocket.

His face solidified into a mask when he saw the three of them staring at him.

After glancing around the crowd, he walked directly to their table, then sat with a heavy thud. Once settled he pointed his weapon at Poindexter from inside his jacket pocket.

Poindexter looked like he might vomit.

"Fancy seeing you again," Dexter said.

"You know what we're doing, right?" the assassin said, his voice low.

"I assume that lump in your jacket pocket isn't there because you're happy to see us," Frisky said.

"I'd rather not create a mess out in public if I don't have to."

"How are you getting back," Frisky said, diverting the topic and realizing he could breathe again.

"That's not something you have to worry about."

Undeterred, Frisky did a moment of personal

grooming, then pressed on. "What I don't understand is why you needed to take Galaxy with us."

The man's grimace said *What do you mean?*

"Get serious, man. I know you're human, but you can't be that dense. If you kill the kid you kill the man, right? So why not just cut out the middleman? Avoid all the weirdness that comes with trying to trick Dexter Galaxy into going with you, and go straight to the source instead? Seems like your way is a lot of complexity for nothing."

The assassin stared at the cat. "I thought you were supposed to be smart."

"I'm much smarter than your average cat," Frisky said. "And your average cat is very smart."

He felt the network of appliances edging closer as he had directed them to. Microwaves adjusted their footpads to carefully edge toward them. Smart cutlery quivered in preparedness. A coffee system gurgled so loudly into overdrive, that Frisky had to send a warning signal to calm down.

The assassin dismissed Frisky with a backhanded wave of his hand.

"I guess it doesn't matter now," he said. "You'll all be dead whenever we leave here."

"So why Galaxy?" Frisky said, goading the assassin.

"We needed him as a compass."

"A compass," Frisky said, contemplating for a moment before continuing in his coolest of cat voices. "I see."

"Maybe *you* see, but I sure as hell don't," Dexter replied.

"Their system can handle the time part of the travel,

but location is another thing. It needed you to come along so it could make a match."

"I guess you're smarter than the average actor, too," the assassin said. "Not that it's much to celebrate, right? Especially an actor scum like Galaxy."

"Hey."

The assassin turned to Galaxy, enjoying the moment even more now.

"People like you don't deserve to live in the same sectors as people like me. You people want to let these mechanical abominations take over the galaxy. You want them to have 'rights' and 'passage' and 'freedom to think on their own.' But people like me know as soon as you do that, life as we know it is over. People like *me* know we can't just let these machines take over, and people like me know people like you are just serving to make matters worse." The assassin barred his teeth and leaned in closer to Dexter. "I admit I find it just grand that we needed your meat, and only your meat, to bring this all to an end."

"Well, I admit I'm not particularly fond of the idea."

"Enough talking," the assassin snapped. His hand pulled the pocket of his jacket forward, and the outline of the plasma gun aimed directly at Poindexter, who remained in a state of Ready to Barf. "Let's get out of here. The quieter we go, the better for all these kids and families."

"We haven't finished our dinners," Dexter said, suddenly petulant.

"Don't be stupid and get all these people killed," the assassin said.

The three of them sat in an awkward silence.

Frisky connected hard to the network to send a message.

"Now!"

The humidifier in the corner blasted off, spewing a stream of high-pressure steam as it flew like a heat-seeking missile.

The assassin stumbled back in his seat as he pulled his weapon, but the humidifier crashed into him, sloshing water from its reservoir across the table, the cascade sending both the food and the table tumbling.

Arg! the assassin called, crashing backward to the floor. His chair skittered away.

The man got up, though, plasma gun still directed at Poindexter, who was frozen in fear. Galaxy's coolness under pressure was apparently a learned trait.

Frisky took the momentary respite as an opening to attack.

He leaped to the assassin and sunk both teeth and claws into his shoulder.

But the man was prepared this time. He rolled and let Frisky's momentum carry him over his shoulder. The cat twisted but there was only so much that 1-g physics allowed, and while his cat instincts were perfectly honed, they only went so far.

Oof!

Frisky crashed to the tiled floor with a thud. He turned, back arched, ears pinned back, and claws at the ready.

In that same motion, the assassin stood tall, drawing his plasma pistol up to take a sight on Poindexter.

The kid was going to die.

Frisky knew it.

THE MAGICAL MYSTERY CRUISE!

Poindexter Steckerman knew it.

The only person who didn't know it was Dexter Galaxy himself, who launched his body into free flight as the assassin pulled the trigger.

The weapon flared scarlet.

A searing blast of smoldering plasma arced through the open dining room, headed directly toward Poindexter's heart. It flew then, clear and true. And Frisky understood all was for naught. The kid was dead. Nothing to be done.

Then—.

As if from nowhere—

Came the flying figure of Dexter Galaxy—.

His arms extended in perfect Superman pose as he flew in front of Poindexter, screaming his fear but leaping into the fray anyway.

The blast struck him with a direct hit, and the actor fell to the floor.

The smell of roasted flesh became overbearing.

The time Dexter bought was just enough, though.

The microwave sprang to Poindexter's aid, propelling itself off the ledge by leveraging its door. It bashed against the assassin's shoulder, knocking him off balance so that he staggered up against the wall. The intelligent cutlery bounced along the server's bar before cartwheeling into a flashing set of restraints that tacked the assassin's jacket to that same wall.

The man laughed, though, and started to rip his arms from the knives.

Amid screams from the now fully understanding visitors, Frisky called in the final reinforcement.

"Now!" Frisky called.

A self-powered ironing board from the Wash part of the conglomeration twirly-birded through the air to crunch hard on the assassin's temple. He fell hard and motionless to the floor. The vending machine and the virtual claw device that were stashed in the corner edged closer until they stood sentry over the motionless figure.

A trickle of blood seeped down the assassin's face from where the ironing board had clipped him.

"I'm not even sorry," the ironing board beeped.

Poindexter and Frisky ran to Dexter.

He lay gasping on the floor, holding his shoulder and chest in obvious pain.

"Are you okay, Dex?" the kid said.

"I'm fine," Galaxy said in a euphoric giggle. "I saved my own life, man. I saved my own life!"

Poindexter grabbed Galaxy's hand. "I can't believe you did this for me."

"I did it for both of us, Poindexter. Don't let me down now, okay? Don't worry about me. There's too much left to do. Save the appliances!"

Dexter faded, his eyes closed, and he slumped into unconsciousness.

"Don't die on me, old man."

Frisky sniffed him.

"He doesn't smell dead."

"You can smell that?"

"Kind of," Frisky said. There was no way to describe what a cat's olfactory system could do to someone who was not a cat. But with Dexter seemingly not dead yet, he could focus on the task at hand.

"This one, though," Frisky said as he jumped to

stand on the assassin's limp form. He sniffed, feeling the leaden sensation of the body. He'd fallen badly. "I think he's seen his last days."

Hoping to find the device the assassin would have used to travel time, Frisky poked paws through his pockets.

Nothing.

Around them, the people who had scattered at the commotion were coming back. Frisky glanced around, suddenly not certain what to do about the pair of unconscious people sprawled over the floor. Outside, someone was calling for help.

"Beep," called the microwave as it used its doors to right itself.

"We've got to get out of here," Frisky said to Poindexter. "Can you carry him?"

"I can try."

"Cover us," Frisky said to the appliances as Poindexter struggled to lift Dexter.

Then they ran.

Frisky, processing, understood they were in serious trouble. How to deal with Dexter Galaxy was important.

But first and foremost, without knowing what the assassin had been doing, Frisky still wasn't sure how to get home.

CHAPTER 12

"And just where do you think we're going?" Lyn said, yanking his arm away as James pushed him along the service corridor. Ahead of them, the tech strode down the hallway at a brisk clip, oblivious to the brothers and obviously still upset at being chewed out by the chief.

"We're following that guy," James huffed. "Just be quiet."

"Why?"

"No time to explain. Just don't lose him."

Lyn stood his ground. "Tell me or we're not going anywhere."

"Jesus, Lyn. Don't be like that." James didn't want to tell his brother anything at all because he didn't trust Lyn *not* to do something stupid like go rushing down the hallway and confront the guy. His brother was unpredictable in most situations but, amped on grief over his lost kitty, Lyn was capable of anything now. "On second thought, never mind," James said as he took in the defiant glare on Lyn's face. "Go ahead and go your own way. I'll see you at the soundcheck."

He pushed Lyn back down the hallway and hurried to chase the tech.

"You can't get away with just leaving me in the cold like that," Lyn said, following James as he pushed down that corridor. "What are you doing?"

"Oh, shush."

"Don't shush me."

James turned a corner the tech had taken. The guy seemed to be headed to the service area. Which made sense. There was almost certainly a trash disintegrator down there. The guy had to get rid of the device.

"Look," James said, giving in. "Promise me you won't do anything stupid, okay?"

"Me? Do something stupid? I'm hurt."

James rolled his eyes as he hustled along. "I didn't want to do it this way, but I do probably need your help."

"Of course, you do!"

James kept a striding pace. "Just promise to be quiet for now and keep your eyes on that technician. I promise to give you the details as soon as I can."

Lyn made a zipping motion across his lips and goggled his eyes into a wild expression as he raced along behind James.

A moment later they came to a large, gaping bay that housed several trash bins that sat on a slowly moving conveyor. James held back and the brothers pressed against the wall before peering into the chamber. The conveyor led to the open gate of a system that whined and zapped as each trash bin rolled through the disintegrator. When each container had finished being processed, it left the system empty and was sent back to the line to be refilled.

An unpleasant odor rolled from the room.

"That's a lot of trash," James whispered to himself.

"A disintegration bin?" Lyn said. "What are we doing at a disintegration bin?"

James made an unhappy motion of zipped lips then turned back to watch the tech, who had been on a direct path to the nearest trash bin but who had been stopped by the huge, Denebian operator who loomed over the tech.

"What are you doing?" the operator demanded.

"I have something that needs to be discarded," the tech replied, pulling the device from his pocket.

The Denebian puffed his chest out and crossed his purple-skinned arms. "You can't add unauthorized trash. Personal refuse can be discarded through normal channels. There are bins at several locations around the ship."

The tech's face grew darker and more agitated. "But I don't want to put this in public bins."

The operator smirked, then took an even more powerful pose that entailed putting both hands on his hips and flexing his not-inconsiderable muscles. "We are very proud of our trash here, buddy. You do it the right way or you don't do it."

"But—"

The operator grabbed the tech by the collar and lifted him. "What part of *we're very proud of our trash* do you not understand?"

The tech, struggling to breathe, pumped his legs like

he was pedaling a non-existent bicycle. His eyes bulged and his breath came in choking gasps.

James felt Lyn's movement beside him, but everything happened too quickly for him to put a hold on him.

"What seems to be the problem here?" Lyn said as he shot past James and came to the pair.

The operator, caught by surprise, dropped the tech back to the floor.

The tech, gasping for breath, adjusted his clothes back to something more comfortable. Once he was breathing properly, he slid the device into his pocket.

"Violation of Refuse Protocol B17," the Denebian operator grunted, then bent in closer to examine Lyn. "Nothing for passengers to be concerned with."

Lyn turned to the tech. "Is this true? Were you in violation of Refuse Protocol B17?"

"Um," the tech said. He was a human, and smaller than Lyn. He glanced at the operator, and then at Lyn.

The operator gave a rough grunt.

The tech backed away a half step. He seemed reluctant to engage. "If this gentleman says I was in violation of protocol B17, I'm sure I was. But it's nothing serious, right? The gentleman was just explaining a procedure we need to follow. I'll be on my way now. Thanks anyhow."

"I'm sure that will be fine by the foreman," Lyn said.

He put his hand on the tech's shoulder and turned him around.

"Isn't that right, foreman?"

Lyn raised an eyebrow at the Denebian, then winked. "We all know you could have popped his head off, but no reason to get fired for someone like that, right?"

The operator drew his eyes into a tight focus and pursed his lips, but eventually nodded with a sagely air of wisdom. "That's right. It's not a problem." He glared at the tech, then shooed him away. "You go along now."

The tech scurred quickly off.

The operator straightened up. "Thank you for your help, human."

Lyn gave a quick salute, then left.

"What was that?" James said as Lyn left the chamber. He chased his brother down the corridor, as the zapping and grinding of the disintegration unit faded behind them.

"I helped you out," Lyn replied.

"Some great help. Now we've lost the guy. I don't know what to do."

Lyn stopped on a dime, then reached into his pocket. "Well, I was thinking you'd maybe want to fiddle around with this for a while." He retrieved the device and held it out to James.

James, two steps further down the hallway, twisted to focus on the small blue box with spindles jutting from various places, and a dial. "How?"

"Just a little magic trick, I'd say?" Lyn said.

"You picked his pocket?"

"I might have picked up a skill or two in my time on the moon, eh? Either that or there was a book cube on magic tricks in the gift shop." His smile was smooth and sly. "Pick whichever answer you like."

Taking his brother in, James took the device.

"All right," he said. "You're forgiven."

CHAPTER 13

Fae Feral stood at their cell's locked doorway, gazing out to the central room of the ship's brig. "What are we doing here, Doozie? We should just flow out, right?"

As shapeshifters, it wouldn't be hard to leave. Just transmute to a spineless gel blob and flow through the cracks in the door. As if to prove it, Fae raised one hand and let it turn into a waving, liquid glob, then recreated the hand and ran it over the pink scales she'd expressed over her now oblong skull.

"That won't help anything," Doozie said. She sat on the hard pallet across the cell, having just finished eating the dinner the crew provided. She expressed extra flesh into her shoulder to make a shrug. "We can't go anywhere else until the ship docks, anyway. No one will let us play the shows. Better to just sit tight and let the captain do what he's going to do."

Fae sighed. "You're right. At least until we get to the next stop. Maybe we get off then?"

"And kill our career?"

"What career, Dooz?" Fae put her head on the crossbar. "Look at us. We're done for, right? No one loves us. Can't catch a break, and when we do it's just a gig for some old has-been who just wants to get his magic wand off. Might as well jump ship when we get the chance."

"Then what? Head back home?"

"Why not?"

"Unfortunately, I can't argue with that."

Doozie stood up and slid her tray into a disposal slot, then put her hand on Fae's shoulder. "You've got it bad, don't you?"

"No. I've got it right."

Doozie let her skin go the shade of blue that showed her sister she understood, and that Fae was almost certainly right. She gazed around, feeling the weight of the locked and barred doors. Even though those locks and bars meant nothing to shapeshifters, their mere presence carried a message from this world.

We don't want you, those bars whispered. *You don't belong here.*

She sighed along with Fae's breathing patterns.

"All right, Fae," Doozie said. "Next stop. Let's go home."

CHAPTER 14

"Let's turn the knob this way," Lyn said, grabbing the device from James's hand.

James yanked it back. "You promised not to do anything stupid."

"Hey! Who got the box to begin with?"

"All right," James said. "Don't do anything *else* stupid."

Sitting in the green room, James's fingers shook with anticipation. He felt jittery with the need to dig into the little blue box because it looked more complex every time he tried to examine it. If he could break it down, he still thought, he could figure out what had happened to Frisky and Dexter Galaxy. If he could do that, then he could spring the sisters from their prison cell.

But he was worried about what would happen if he twirled the wrong knob in the wrong way, and there hadn't been time to do the examination justice.

Now it was showtime.

He brushed his hands down the thigh of his stage pants, a bright red pair of cargo leggings with sonic pressure pads built into them that gave an entirely new meaning to the term *playing in your pants*.

"Agh," he said, shaking his fingers off and seeing clumps of fur slowly fall to the floor. "Ever since we got hold of that creature, I'm nothing but a ball of cat hair."

"Yeah," Lyn said with a sigh. "I miss the little bugger, too."

The rumble of fans clamoring outside the green room let James know they were ready, which was nice. It was good to be wanted. But mostly James knew that anything less than being exactly on time from here on out would cause Calista Parallax to fire them on the spot. And like it or not, Parallax was growing a name in the business. Pissing her off would have consequences.

The Intergalactic Band of Brilliance had to go on stage, and they had to go on now.

That meant he had no time for the device.

To make matters worse, the boys had to split up immediately after the show in order to play both the Feral Sisters' event and Frisky's gig.

That *Marvel* would be docking a few hours after their last gig probably worked in their favor. At least the passengers were buzzing about magical tours to Aldebaran's various moons, meaning that attention spans were not at their peak.

Despite himself, his new song "Sabrina Katrina" ran through James's head.

He smiled then.

Yes.

If you don't have time, make time.

It was a phrase their first guitar teacher used to push them to practice.

Maybe, just maybe, they could get away with a bit of entertainment sleight-of-hand on this Magical Mystery Cruise.

"I've got an idea," he said to his brother, suddenly feeling excited. "I need time to dig into this thing. And you can give it to me."

"Do tell on, then, Mac James."

"First, I need to teach you this song."

"Is it 'Sabrina Katrina'?"

"That's the one."

"Ha! The girls really got their hooks into you, don't they?"

"I think it's going to be a hit," James said, his enthusiasm coming through his rapid voice. The full truth of the moment built inside him as he spoke. So strongly he didn't know why he hadn't seen it earlier. "But we need to play it now so we can tell everyone how great they are, and how the ship is holding them like animals for no good reason. Every gig. Both when we're together and when we're alone. Give an introduction that lets people know this is our homage to the amazing Feral Sisters."

"You mean we play the sympathy card?"

"More like the justice card than the sympathy card, but whatever."

"I like this side of you, brother. You should let it out more often."

Ignoring Lyn, James plowed on. Outside the room, swelling voices began to chant for the Intergalactic BoB.

"This is important, all right? We need to get it right."

"Hmm. All right."

"Here it is," James said as he picked up his guitar. "Focus on the solo at the end, all right?"

"All right."

James hit the band system and began playing.

The show goes on, in a smoky dim lit room
The crowd wants a thrill, let out a roar when the lights
go down
There are fanboys, and there are skeptics
Some want to know how you do it, some just want to drink
the night away

You move majestic, shape shifting in the air
Change from red to blue, skin to scale, right on cue
I would come undone, without you around
You've got the grace of Monaco like a model in a magazine

Sabrina Katrina
You make me feel like a millionaire, Ya!
Sabrina Katrina
Make me feel like I'm floating on air, Ya!

Sabrina Katrina
You make me feel like a millionaire, Ya!
Sabrina Katrina

THE MAGICAL MYSTERY CRUISE!

Make me feel so serene, Ya!

Slick magic tricks, and sleight of hand
Give the people what they want, and they'll come back again
and again again
As you raise the curtain, crowd unaware
Dressed in sparkle wear, you pass the key and trip the
trap door

Sabrina Katrina
You make me feel like a millionaire, Ya!
Sabrina Katrina
Make me feel like I'm floating on air, Ya!

Sabrina Katrina
You make me feel like a millionaire, Ya!
Sabrina Katrina
Make me feel so serene, Ya!

I would come undone
I would come undone
I would come undone
I would come undone
I would come undone

I would come undone

"I love it," Lyn said when James was finished. "So what about the solo?"

"I need you to play it, and by play it, I mean, really play it."

Lyn frowned, but James continued without hesitation.

"I'm thinking twenty minutes. Maybe more. You can do that, right? Shred for a half hour?"

Lyn's expression grew belligerent. "*I* can shred forever." Then dawning came, and Lyn's smile glowed nebula-bright. "You mean I shred while you step off the stage for a bit of a break?"

James's grin matched his brother's.

It was a classic play. One member runs on a huge solo to give the rest of the band time to get a drink or do whatever needful things needed to be done.

"A guy gets tired, you know?" James quipped. "Sometimes he needs a little rest."

Lyn gave an exaggerated head nod.

"Think you can pull it off?" James said, challenging.

"Just watch me."

Outside, the fans began to stomp in unison.

James dropped the device into a drawer, then covered it up and shoved it far into the back before closing it up.

"Let's go, then," he said. "Time to put on a bit of magic."

CHAPTER 15

At least Dexter Galaxy didn't smell dead.

Not yet, anyway. But Frisky wasn't sure how much longer that was going to last.

He glanced over his shoulder to see the actor was still being carried by Poindexter.

The kid gasped under the actor's weight, the limp body slung partially over one shoulder, arms and legs dangling this way and that as Poindexter fought gravity, momentum, and a distinct lack of muscle. Rivers of perspiration streamed down the kid's forehead, and — since the day was still hot — the flush of his exertion highlighted his acne.

"I can't believe I weigh so much," Poindexter groaned as one of Dexter Galaxy's legs flopped against his chest.

They had left the Eat, Play, Wash and were taking a direct route to where Frisky's surveillance feeds had said the assassin had spent time recovering from his first unsuccessful attempt at killing Poindexter. With luck, the man had stashed something away that would let them get home.

If so, Frisky would figure it out.

He was, as noted, smarter than the average cat.

That's what he was thinking as they trotted into a small park with a pair of benches set around the edges of a circular plaza, which in turn was surrounded by a sparsely spaced ring of trees. A patch of real grass grew at its center.

Ahchoo!

Frisky gave a massive sneeze.

"Damn it."

Poindexter cried with happiness at the sight of the bench.

Struggling mightily now, he almost made it all the way to the first bench before the actor's form slipped from his grasp to thud heavily onto the bricked plaza.

"I'm sorry!" Poindexter exclaimed as he stood over Galaxy's slumped form. His hands raised to wrap around his head. "Oh, my hells, man. I'm sorry!" He grabbed Galaxy's hand and dragged him toward the bench, then dropped it like it had suddenly gotten hot. "I am so, so sorry!"

"Ahchooo!"

Frisky's eyes were watering, again. Nothing was worse than a cat with hay fever.

He could feel his sniffer swelling up. It made him wonder how much longer it would be dependable, and what that might mean for his ability to know if Dexter Galaxy was still alive or not.

The Nearest Human Repair Center is .526 kilometers down Audubon Rideway, a warm-throated feline voice came across Frisky's connection as if to answer his concern.

Frisky yelped in surprise. "No time for that. Search this place!"

He didn't want to think about what would happen to Galaxy if they couldn't get back to their own time. Who knew how medical procedures were done here in the barbaric past, and even if they got done here, how would such procedures fare in a time warp?

The assassin had to have a backdoor, right?

He had to have a way back to the future or he wouldn't have come.

Not sure what he was looking for, Frisky leaped up to the closest bench.

Perhaps it would be a box. Or a card. Or a chip of some kind?

He pressed a paw into every nook, crease, and corner, sniffing and peering into places a human couldn't see, whiskers flexing. He fed the flow from his optical nerves through a *Virtch-U-Find* decoder that was part of a nearby surveillance system his network had connected to. The process enhanced every view of the area, but it revealed nothing.

He peered into a final crack in the bench seat.

How small could the return device be?

Grain of sand?

Should they go back to the Eat, Play, Wash to do a more thorough inspection of the comatose assassin?

His first pass had been done quickly and under no little duress, so he could have missed something. But the idea of returning felt like a bad idea now. No one wanted to get caught up in the mess of an inquiry from law enforcement that exists out of their time.

Better to look here.

There was nothing on this bench, though.

Poindexter, having left Galaxy lying on the brick plaza, was on hands and knees now, picking his way around the perimeter of the brick and pressing his sweat-lined nose down into his search. "I wish we had a detector," he said as he disappeared into the tiny copse of elm trees.

Frisky leaped to the backrest of the bench he was on, then bent to examine the support structure. Could the assassin have stashed the return trigger here?

He saw nothing.

As he padded to the other bench three officer systems arrived, each clad in silvery uniforms that reflected the sun's light and made Frisky blink. Coppers! Crap. Just what they didn't need.

They were tall and moved with precise strides that allowed them to pass for human, but that even a moderate examination revealed came from autonomous mechanicals with AI cognitives.

Frisky's wireless connection bounced off them at first.

"Old protocols. Damn it!"

He stifled a hiss and, giving a low growl, instead tried to search his memories.

"Where the hell is *Marvel* when you want him?"

"Excuse me," the lead officer said with a smile that also blazed in the sun, "but did you just arrive from the Eat, Play, Wash Grill and Fun Room?" They pointed to where Poindexter had left the actor sprawled on the ground. "And what's this gentleman doing?"

Frisky meowed a reply. *No hables human,* right?

"Because we have reports of a feline and two male suspects heading this way, but there is only the two of you here."

"I found something." It was Poindexter stepping back onto the open plaza. He was shaking dirt from a tiny box of some kind. Recognizing the officers, he drew up abruptly and palmed the box. His cheeks grew cherry red.

"And what is that, young man?" the officer said. "Please provide your evidence to enable proper Law Enforcement activities to commence."

One of the backup officers presented an open palm to Poindexter.

Before Poindexter could react, Frisky leaped to the supporting officer's palm, planted his butt in the officer's hand, and began to rub his jaws and cheeks against the silvery shoulder of their uniform jacket. No way was he letting Poindexter give the office that box. The officer, perplexed, instinctively reached his other hand up to scratch Frisky on the top of his head. Bearing it, Frisky's mind found the information he needed to adjust his wireless protocols to match these older variants inside the officers. The link with the leader fell together with a satisfying thrum.

"We were just wondering, officer," Frisky said, stalling for time as he worked to get the hang of the ancient command structure. "Do you know how to get to San Jose?"

"San Jose?"

"There is a tram there, right?"

"Um. Yes. There is. But—"

Frisky twitched a whisker toward Poindexter. "My friend here said he had directions, but he's been away so long I'm afraid he's lost the trail."

"I see. Um."

Frisky packaged up a new comm packet and sent it through the officer's interface. *Suspects seen on Preston and Phillips. All units give chase.*

All three officers' eyes flickered in a series of blinks.

"Come along then," the lead officer said.

They turned in unison and as Frisky jumped to the ground, they stepped briskly away.

A moment later, Poindexter took a deep, relaxing breath and looked at Frisky with wide eyes. "How did you do that?"

"I thought you were the expert at talking to intelligent appliances."

"Um."

"Don't worry, kid," Frisky said, seeing the confusion on Poindexter's face, and understanding that perhaps his friend Joe was the real brains behind the effort. He twitched a whisker toward Galaxy's motionless form. "I think the existence of that galoot over there alone says you'll figure it out soon enough."

"Yeah, maybe Joe will let me hang around his garage a little more."

"Probably a good idea."

"Aaaaagh." From his place on the plaza, Dexter Galaxy gave a painful groan as he rolled over, regaining some form of consciousness.

Frisky wasted no time padding directly to Poindexter.

"Let's get going. If we're going to save the idiot, it's probably time we see if that little box in your hand can send us back to our own timeline."

Poindexter nodded, then knelt.

The box covered most of his palm. Black and slim. It appeared dense if not heavy. Even the weakling kid hefted it without problem. Clods of dirt and peat from the tree roots still clung to its surface, which was smooth and without anything that resembled a knob, dial, setting, or control panel. Not even a light blinking.

It was nothing at all like the device Frisky had seen in Altair the All-Knowing's Chaos Contraption before it had zapped them back here to the past.

"What is it?" Poindexter said.

Frisky sniffed it.

Truth dawned.

"It's a brick," Frisky said.

"A brick?"

"Yeah," Frisky said, mind racing. "Probably just a buried surveillance device. Nothing but sensors if it was working."

Alas, useful or not, it was dead now.

"Aaaagh," Dexter called again, clearly in pain.

A weird sensation came over Frisky. A foreign feeling that draped over him like a heavy blanket. He wasn't sure exactly what it was.

No.

That was wrong.

He knew exactly what it was, but his brain couldn't accept it.

Failure.

That's what it was.

He'd been with the Moore brothers long enough that he was familiar with the concept. But now, for the first time in his life, the raw, rancid essence of failure clotted up his own throat so full of cotton that he didn't think he could even look at Poindexter and utter the famous words "I meant to do that."

Instead, Frisky felt cold fingers of dread wrapping themselves around his chest and piercing the inner elements of his solar plexus.

Dexter Galaxy's next moan felt harsh and painful.

Through it all, Frisky came to understand something in a way he'd not considered before.

He was alone now.

The assassin hadn't had a way back.

"We are locked here," Frisky said, his voice wavering in a most uncatlike way.

CHAPTER 16

James had to hand it to his brother.

When the ending bars of "Sabrina Katrina" came around, Lyn stepped up, grabbed Victoria — his favorite guitar — by the fretboard, and proceeded to give her a workout the likes he hadn't seen in a long time.

James had barely stepped off the stage, and already the house was going crazy over Lyn's guitar-tastic acrobatics.

His heart thumped as, holding his own axe as balance, James raced down the few steps through the stage hallway and back to the green room. The gig had been amazing. From "Let's Disappear," to "Ants in My Guitar," and "Frisky," the crowd loved it all. And then, the *coup de gras* was their introduction to "Sabrina Katrina," which had played up the girls, and which had drawn boos and groans at all the right parts when he described how they were being incarcerated unjustly.

"Free the girls!" Lyn had burst in to yell.

And the crowd took up the chant, stomping their

feet and clapping as they called *Free the girls! Free the girls! Free the girls!*

Now Lyn had them in the palm of his hand, playing a lead that James knew would burn the house down.

The door snapped shut behind him.

He dropped his guitar on the couch against the longer wall and pulled a drawer from the vanity. There. The device. He sat down, trying to calm himself so his hands didn't shake. His chest heaved with exertion.

"Not helping!" he said to himself.

With a deep breath, he grabbed the device firmly.

His hands were dripping in sweat, so he dried one, then the other off on his pants again, once again, grimacing as they came back with a thin layer of Frisky's gray fur.

Dumb cat.

He sat the box on the vanity counter and let bright light from the panes along the mirrored wall illuminate it.

Nubs remained where three physical wires had been cut.

He was a musician, not a computer scientist, though. They had connected to something, obviously, but he wasn't sure what.

He pushed a button and multicolored lights flashed a power-up sequence. So the nubs were probably data feeds of some kind.

Two discs were recessed into the surface of what James took for the top of the device.

James reached a finger out, and twirled one to the left, then to the right, and back again.

They seemed to be settings of some sort.

THE MAGICAL MYSTERY CRUISE!

Along the bottom of the dials were three buttons. A red one, a blue one, and a green one.

If he was right, it made sense these would be some kind of controllers.

When he looked along the sides of the device, small camera lenses greeted him.

"Interestinger and interestinger," he mumbled.

A booming slam on the door behind him about made him pee his pants.

"What are you doing in there, you idiot!"

Calista Parallax.

Damn it.

"Get out there with your brother or you're fired!"

"Just a minute!"

He stared at the box.

If he was right about the dials, they were probably set in the same way they had been when Galaxy and the cat disappeared. And if the device had loaded everything from the data feeds it needed to load in order to do its thing, maybe it would work anyway. The question that raced through James's mind was this.

Which button?

Red? Blue? Green?

It was now or never. Or at least it was now or many days from now, which might as well be never as far as it came to saving Frisky. Assuming the cat was even savable.

And it might as well be now or never as far as the sisters were concerned.

He recalled the painfully beautiful expression of despair on Fae Feral's face as they were being interrogated.

He imagined them both locked in their cell, as he and Lyn had been locked up last trip.

And, he recalled the sensation of watching their act up close.

With these memories washing over him, an overwhelming urge to know the truth came over James.

Another round of fevered banging came at the door.

"I swear to all the gods that you and your brother are never working again!"

Red seemed like a universal Stop Sign. So that wasn't it.

So, blue or green?

His finger hovered over the green button. Green for go.

No.

That wouldn't be right either, would it? If green was for go, then maybe blue was for return. And that's what he needed here, right? Return. Bring the actor and the cat back.

It was all so confusing.

He noted another stray cat hair clinging to his sweaty finger and tried unsuccessfully to flick it off.

In the distance, his brother wailed on Vicky. He really was quite good.

The banging came again, this time hard enough to shake the room.

Now, he thought. It had to be now. This was why he was here.

"Free the girls!" he called.

With a single motion, James jammed his thumb on the blue button.

CHAPTER 17

Lyn Moore stood at the edge of the stage. He was in a state of total bliss, wailing on Victoria like he'd never wailed before.

The crowd had been chanting *Free the Girls* on endless loop.

Lyn was pouring triplets and chords and bends into the space between their voices. He'd done a full minute of staccato tap shredding and done percussion strums on Vicky's solid body with his hips, shoulders, elbows, and maybe parts of the body better left unsaid.

He was in the zone.

Vicky was in the zone.

And the people.

Oh.

The people. He danced in front of three Zendaks all wearing violet fringed laser jackets, fell back into a mosh pit that had properly pushed him back onto the stage to hammer out a whammy-wand skeed that had everyone crying with ecstasy, their faces tilted up in a mix of glee and anger that Lyn knew he might never see on stage again. One of Vickie's strings broke, but he adjusted in real-time.

James was right.

"Sabrina Katrina" was the right song at the right time.

A true hit.

Feeling the time was right for a change of pace, Lyn stepped up to the artificial gravity microphone with intent to scat.

As he opened his mouth, though, a flash of light erupted.

Time seemed to stop.

The light, so blinding and sharp Lyn thought the place might have gone nova, brought everything to a halt.

Lyn screamed then, as did everyone else, raising his hand to protect himself, and seeing the outline of his own bones shining through the glare.

―――

What the hells? Frisky thought.

One minute he was standing in the park plaza with the pimply-faced Poindexter Steckerman, and the next he was on stage?

Feeling the hard boards under his paws, Frisky blinked and, with his stomach feeling suddenly putrid, hacked up a hairball right there in front of Lyn.

It made him feel better.

Or at least it made him feel well enough and grounded enough that he could take in his surroundings.

THE MAGICAL MYSTERY CRUISE!

People were looking at him, their gazes a mass of confusion and fear, several with hands covering their eyes or their ears.

A hushed silence hung in the expanse, too. Which seemed as weird as he felt.

From across the stage, Dexter Galaxy again whimpered in pain.

The sound brought everything into a final focus.

Lyn Moore stood slack-jawed by the floating microphone, sweating profusely as his chest heaved in exertion. His guitar was slung over his shoulder. A single string looped from its head, waving in random patterns brought out by the Coriolis effect that the stage used for part of its gravity.

James burst in from the side stage, one fist clenched around the neck of his own starburst instrument, the other holding the device Frisky recognized was from the Chaos Contraption.

The woman, Calista Parallax, her bright face as red as her flowing tunic, was right behind.

Frisky glanced at the wet hairball between his feet.

"I meant to do that," he said.

A chuckle was the first sound heard. Then full laughter.

Inside his brain, Frisky felt connections reform.

Glad to sense you again, Marvel said through their links. *Where were you?*

Frisky was never so happy to hear a star cruiser in his whole life.

"They're back!" someone yelled from the back of the room. "Dexter Galaxy and Frisky are back!"

With that, the entire room erupted in cheers.

Fuming, Calista Parallax caught up with James. "I suggest you turn in your employee pass cube and go quietly," she said between clenched jaws.

"You're firing the wrong guy," James replied.

The device was still warm in his hand.

"Believe me, I'm firing your brother, too." She glared at Lyn.

"I mean that you need to be firing the security director," James said.

"Officer Jabbert?"

"Though really you'll need to get him arrested first."

"What?"

James held up the device to waggle it before her but focused instead on the struggling form of Dexter Galaxy. He raced immediately to the actor's side.

"Call the medical bay," he said when he arrived. "This man's been shot!"

EPILOGUE

Two very hectic days later, the boys sat at the pool again, this time in the quiet of the crew section, though, and this time joined by the Feral Sisters, their chaise lounges arranged in a big "plus sign," feet to the center.

In hopes of making the boys more comfortable, both sisters were expressing human body constructs, Fae dark-skinned and blonde, Doozie light-skinned and red. Even though the girls' suits were modest for the time, their appearance was attractive enough that they were failing miserably at making the boys comfortable.

None of them seemed to mind.

James, as always, strummed his guitar, picking out a new idea.

"Do you ever go anywhere without that?" Doozie chided him.

Blushing a shade, James shrugged.

Frisky lapped a fresh Meow Tai and lounged on a warm spot on the table right in the middle of them all.

Lyn and Fae were occupied waving to fans across the way.

In those two very hectic days since James had hit the blue button to retrieve Frisky and Dexter Galaxy from the actor's past, Galaxy had of course been the main story. But there was plenty of attention to slop over to them. As a big star already, Dexter Galaxy was familiar with the pressures of that kind of fame. The boys and the sisters were not. Between the debrief to the captain, the activity around Security Officer Jabbert's arrest, and the reporters and paparazzi, the siblings had been worn to such a frazzle that they barely had energy for the flat-out adoration of the fans who came to their shows.

This moment sitting in the crew section of *Marvel*'s enormous pool ring was the first quiet time any of the five had gotten together since that moment.

Fae's fannish flirtations aside, the girls were particularly appreciative of the quiet space that came with being on the crew deck.

"It makes me sad that Officer Jones wasn't even a real officer," Fae said, staring at her feet while she flexed her toes. "He was so easy on the eyes."

"How did you figure that out, James?" Doozie asked. "That Jones wasn't Jones?"

"I didn't. Or at least not until after the fact. But I should have known it the moment Lyn said that the key was to find him."

"I did?" Lyn said. He took a sip of the effervescent Caboom tonic he'd ordered.

"Yes, Lyn, you did."

"So, it's almost like *I* solved the case?"

"Only if by *almost* you mean *not*."

THE MAGICAL MYSTERY CRUISE!

"Yeah," Frisky said. "I'm the one who went through the records and found that *Jones*'s real name, Phineas Brookins, had a record."

In fact, Brookins had a quite-long string of offenses on his record, starting back when he was a preteen, and trailing all the way through his time joining the largest galactic crime syndicate in the known universe.

Officer Jabbert had been on the take to that syndicate and had conspired to sneak Brookins, aka Lucifrous Jones, onto the cruise.

Fae used her big toe to scratch Frisky on the jaw.

He allowed it and purred only a little.

"I still don't know why they cared so much about intelligent kitchen appliances getting their rights. Wanting to kill Dexter seems a little extreme," Fae said.

"When you add up every star in the galaxy, there's a lot of money in kitchen appliances," James replied.

"And you don't want the help getting any ideas," Frisky quipped.

"But I still can't believe they would time-jump all the way to Galaxy's past. Why not just kill him now?"

"Because he's a big star now, silly," Fae's sister replied. "He's got a whole entourage with him. Do you know how hard it is to get through that?"

"I assume you tried?"

Doozie raised her eyebrow suggestively. "And you haven't?"

"Whatever," Fae shrugged. "Besides, they're a master crime syndicate. Don't tell me they can't do anything they want."

"Of course, they can," James said. "But that cat's out of the bag," he said with a nod to Frisky. "Intelligent freezers are getting their personal rights all over the place today, so killing Galaxy in the now doesn't solve anything."

"Yes, right," Lyn added, rubbing his chin sagely. "Everything is already too much out of control."

James bit his tongue.

Once Frisky had uncovered the identity of Lucifrous Jones everything had fallen into place for him. He had already laid out the full plot when they briefed the captain earlier. The syndicate had arranged to have "Lucifrous Jones" convince the sisters to bring Galaxy into the magic act, then he made additions to the washed-up magician's Chaos Contraption. Then when Altair did his thing, "Jones" stepped in at just the right time to send them both back to Galaxy's childhood. The idea had been that once the assassin had finished the job, every bit of social progress the appliances had won would disappear into the ether of the multiverse, every appliance would be dumb again, and no one would be wiser.

Jabbert would engage the device again to bring "Jones" back to the present.

Voila!

Things would just move on.

But Frisky mucked everything up with his surprise leap, and then the tech had inadvertently broken the plan completely by removing the time machine's triggering device.

Worried that everything was going haywire when Jabbert saw what he assumed was the broken device, he ordered the thing disintegrated—which would have left all three of the travelers stranded in time.

THE MAGICAL MYSTERY CRUISE!

"Good thing Frisky's fur sheds," Lyn said, still rubbing his chin.

Just as the syndicate had needed Dexter Galaxy's DNA to connect today's Dexter with yesterday's Poindexter, it had been that cat hair that clung to James's pants, then to his hands as he pushed the button that made the connection to Frisky across time.

"That's right," Doozie said with a light peal of laughter. "I'd hate to have lost the little guy."

"Whadday mean, *little guy?*"

"Sorry about that."

"He *is* big for a cat," Fae replied.

In a slow wave, Frisky blinked his green eyes at Fae. "You may continue to scratch my back," he said.

James laughed. "Yeah. Just be careful. Cat fur gets everywhere, and I'm not sure I want to know what happens if you shift around it."

Across the expanse of the pool sector, cruisegoers gathered, pointing at them, and taking photos. Some seemed to jump up and down on tentacles, legs, and other appendages.

"It's like they've all forgotten Altair the All-Knowing even exists," Lyn said.

Frisky licked a paw and cleaned a talon. "No big loss as far as I'm concerned."

"The guy *was* a bit of a blowhard, wasn't he?" James said. "He was so pissed off when the press reported Galaxy's loss as if it was his fault."

"Well, it was his fault, wasn't it?" Lyn said. "The guy didn't know his trick."

"Touché," James said. He ran his fingers down the fretboard of his guitar, picking a quiet lead that played under the piped-in music. "I'd guess he's pretty much done for now. I hear no respectable place will book him."

Lyn nodded. "That's what I hear, too. Almost feel sorry for the geezer."

"I don't," Fae said, her voice cold.

Indiscriminate voices across the pool muddled together into a gauzy wave of sound. A song. They were singing "Kiss the Widow Goodnight," one of the Feral Sisters' most unforgettable pieces. They played it over a laser show complete with a holographic stage piece that included Fae and Doozie riding in cones of artificial gravity while they played and sang.

The thing was a masterpiece as far as James was concerned.

It had brought the house down each of the last two nights.

"I can't believe this is happening," Fae said, ripping her gaze away from the throng of fans and to first James, then Lyn. She raised her Vumi highball to the boys, its color the perfect shade of amber, then took a sip. "Thank you."

"Yeah. You guys really did us a solid," Doozie seconded the motion with her own highball. "Thank you both."

"Ah, it was nothing," James replied, admittedly still a bit starstruck being this close to the Feral Sisters.

"Sabrina Katrina" was playing all over the place now, and with the publicity that came from being both blazingly good at making multidimensional megamedia art, MDMM for short, and having been railroaded for something they hadn't done, Feral Sisters shows had been sold out for the past two days. It was the break they needed. Now that they'd gotten it, James knew deepest space was the limit for them.

Even if no one else would say it, the sisters were destined to be huge stars.

And, after having spent so long idolizing their shows, James felt strange to be actual friends with them now.

Or, maybe even more than friends, he thought, becoming intensely aware that Doozie was giving him the eye again, something he'd sensed from the moment they'd gotten here. With Fae and Lyn having always seemed to be a thing, he felt awkward.

"Don't say it was nothing, brother," Lyn said. "That song rips, and the intro you gave it that first time set everything in motion."

"What he said," Doozie added.

Lyn reached his own drink from the stand beside his lounge. "To all of us," he said, raising a toast. "Wherever the space wind takes us, eh?"

They all raised glasses, then drank.

Frisky lapped at his Meow Tai.

"About that space wind," Doozie said. "Fae and I have a proposal."

Lyn sat up.

James stopped strumming his guitar.

"First, we've got a little news," Doozie said. "Calista has signed us to a big tour. Seventeen stops around the galaxy, including two nights at the Mirage Belt."

Lyn gave an appreciative whistle.

"That's great," James said. His stomach dropped a little though. They were going to lose the Feral Sisters even sooner than he thought they would. "I hope you'll remember us when you're big stars."

Fae boggled her eyes. "Don't go all dopey on us, James."

"What do you mean?"

"What Fae means, dummy, is that with 'Sabrina Katrina' doing so great, we know the Intergalactic Band of Brilliance is going to be huge, too."

James grimaced, but Doozie wasn't letting him off the hook that easy.

"You know that's true, right? Tell me you see how much the fans love it, and how when you play it they want more."

James nodded. It was true, of course. But ... "It's nothing like you guys are –"

"So, we were thinking that we should team up. You know?"

She waited.

Lyn was the first to totally catch on.

"You want us to tour with you?"

"Yeah," Doozie said, glancing at Fae for final confirmation, and receiving a nod back. "We think you're great, and that it could be fun if we put our two sets together."

James looked at Lyn.

Then at Fae.

And, finally at Doozie.

There was something deeper in her gaze, now. Something that made *him* think that *she* thought that maybe he might *also* be very bendy.

"I, um," James stammered.

"I hate to be the bearer of bad news, brothers, but

it's ix-nay on the our-tay for you," Frisky said, sitting upright and beaming with that essence of certainty that every cat comes equipped with.

"What?" James said. "Why can't we go on tour?"

"Because," the voice of Calista Parallax came from behind them.

She breezed into the area, dressed in casual clothes now, but carrying a tray of fresh drinks for them all.

Parallax stepped through the gathering of chaise lounges and set the tray on the table.

"Just as the Feral Sisters have signed with me, Frisky is now fully under contract with Parallax Entertainments. I've got him lined up as the headliner on the next GCL cruise with the stipulation that the Intergalactic BoB will be his support group. Given that I've made GCL an offer they won't be able to refuse for your contract, too, I thought it would be a grand idea to buy all my clients a round."

She reached down and grabbed a Zendak martini, then raised the glass.

"So, here's to 'Sabrina Katrina,' and all of us getting rich, eh?"

"I don't know," James said, still getting his head around things.

"Come now, boys, don't be so glum. You and the girls can make a band together later. And when that happens it will be even better because then all three of you will be multi-planet stars. Combining them will be even bigger news than Dexter Galaxy coming back from the past."

"I don't know," James said.

"The money will roll in. Trust me."

"Another cruise?" Lyn moaned.

"Cowboys this time!" Frisky purred. "Yee-haw and pass the lariats!"

James sighed.

Their new manager put her glass out. "Here's to us," she said.

Reluctantly, the brothers and sisters joined her.

Over the pool section, a voice spoke.

"Gentlecreatures from all the worlds, I'm so happy to be able to break a new single that I just know is going to be a huge hit. And even better, the singer will be in the Blues Club tonight singing it! Be sure to catch it while you can … presenting 'I'm Back,' by our own amazing talent Frisky the Cat!"

"What?" James said.

A wry smile crossed over Calista Parallax's face. "Didn't Frisky tell you? I licensed his new song to the Galactic Cruise Lines Broadcasting Network."

"Holy …"

"It's gonna be a huge hit," she purred. "Exclusive deal. Not a lot of money, of course, but great exposure."

Both boys sat back then, resigned.

Throughout the section, Frisky's song played.

Across the pool, the fans cheered.

I hear you planned a service
Sent flowers, gifts, and a card
Were you nervous?
That you wouldn't have the heart, and fall apart

Would you say you missed me?
Would you say you cried in the dark?
Did you look to find me?
Did you track prints to find a mark, on a lark

We'll I'm back better than ever
Smarter more clever than I've ever been before
I'm back better then ever
Stronger more handsome than you'll ever be my friends
I'm Back!

You can take it easy
All is fine now rest assured
Your hero's back before you
Spreading joy I'm so demure, that's insured

We'll I'm back better than ever
Smarter more clever than I've ever been before
I'm back better then ever
Stronger more handsome than you'll ever be my friends
I'm Back!

Cat sarcasm that's what I do
Furballs and alcohol I give to you

When it comes to danger I've got you beat
I've got nine lives take a seat
1 2 3 4 5 6 7 8 9….. whoa Nellie!

I'm back better than ever
Smarter more clever than I've ever been before
I'm back better then ever
Stronger more handsome than you'll ever be my friends
I'm Back!

Would you say you missed me?
Would you say you cried in the dark?

YOU'VE REACHED THE END!

We hope you've enjoyed the raucous cruise through the galaxy! If you have, you might find other books in the series to be equally as fun.

Also, if you enjoyed this book, your review on the book retailer of your choice is a great way to help us out. Even a quick line or two can help!

Thank you so much for reading our work!

ACKNOWLEDGMENTS

We would like to thank all the people who have helped us make it this far in life—but, man, that would be a nearly infinite list. Instead, let's narrow it a little. Thanks to all the sets of Collins brothers who came before us. Thanks to Dad, especially, for hanging around while we were brainstorming a bit.

Thanks, too, to Kristine Kathryn Rush, Dean Wesley Smith, and Lisa Silverthorne for throwing their own ideas at us when we asked for a bit of advice. That was a fun lunch.

Thanks to our beta readers, Sharon Bass and John Bodin. You two are the bestest.

Thanks, also, to Karen and Lisa for not laughing at us when we decided to take a flier at this silliness—with special focus on Lisa for being our last reader!

And, finally, thanks to the many airplanes that flew over our recording studio as we were grabbing the audio version of this book. Or, um, actually, no thanks there. Those planes were a real pain.

ABOUT RON & JEFF COLLINS

Jeff and Ron Collins—the original Cruise Brothers—first played music together as youthful teens down in the basement of their home in Louisville, Kentucky. *("No grass, but a lotta grapes!"* - inside Mom joke, there*)*. While occasionally annoying the family and their beloved cat Frisky with boisterous songs at 2am, there were some gems that have managed to stand the test of time (a few even found their way into this Cruise Brothers series).

Then Jeff fiddled around with theater and improv comedy before hightailing it out to Los Angeles to become a rock star, and Ron found his way through engineering and into the life of a high-powered icon in the science fiction field.

Or something like that.

Now here they are. Back, better than ever.

Aside from composing and producing original works, these days you can find Jeff playing live with several tribute bands, including a tribute to Genesis (Gabble Ratchet), Alice Cooper (Pretties For You), and Jane's Addiction (Jane's Addicted).

Ron's short fiction has received a Writers of the Future prize and a CompuServe HOMer Award. His short story "The White Game" was nominated for the Short Mystery Fiction Society's 2016 Derringer Award.

With his daughter, Brigid, he edited the anthology *Face the Strange.*

You can follow Ron at his website: Typosphere.com
Or join Ron's Readers and get two free books!
typosphere.com/newsletter/

ALSO BY RON COLLINS

<u>Novels</u>

Stealing the Sun (9 books)

Saga of the God-Touched Mage (8 books)

Fairies & Fastballs w/Brigid Collins (3 books)

The PEBA Diaries (2 books)

The Knight Deception

Wakers

<u>Collections</u>

Holiday Hope

They Came Back

Collins Creek (Vol 1) Contemporary Currents and Historical Eddies

Collins Creek (Vol 2) Streams of Speculation

Collins Creek (Vol 3) Tides of Adventure

Tomorrow in All the Worlds

Picasso's Cat & Other Stories

Five Magics

<u>Novella</u>

The Bridge to Fae Realm

<u>Poetry</u>

Five Seven Five (100 SF Haiku)

www.ingramcontent.com/pod-product-compliance
Ingram Content Group UK Ltd.
Pitfield, Milton Keynes, MK11 3LW, UK
UKHW041930131224
452403UK00001B/17